Death in Spring

Death in Spring

Translated from the Catalan by Martha Tennent

MERCÈ RODOREDA

With an introduction by Colm Tóibín

PENGUIN BOOKS

This translation is dedicated to Lawrence Venuti and Dolors Juanola.

PENGUIN BOOKS

UK | USA | Canada | Ireland | Australia
India | New Zealand | South Africa

Penguin Books is part of the Penguin Random House group of companies
whose addresses can be found at global.penguinrandomhouse.com.

First published in Catalan as *La mort i la primavera* 1986
This translation first published in the United States of America by Open Letter Books 2009
First published in Great Britain with a new introduction in Penguin Books 2018
001

Text copyright © Institut d'Estudis Catalans
Translation copyright © Martha Tennent, 2009
Originally published in Catalan as *La mort i la primavera* 1986
Introduction copyright © The Heather Blazing, 2018

The moral right of the copyright holders has been asserted

Published by arrangement with Open Letter Books
Translation of this novel was made possible thanks to the support of the Ramon Llull Institut

Set in 11/13 pt Bembo Book MT Std
Typeset by Jouve (UK), Milton Keynes
Printed in Great Britain by Clays Ltd, St Ives plc

A CIP catalogue record for this book is available from the British Library

ISBN: 978-0-241-35254-0

www.greenpenguin.co.uk

Introduction

In some societies, language is a way to restrain experience, take it down to a level where it might stay. It is neither ornament nor exaltation; it is firm and austere in its purpose. It is thus a form of calm, modest knowledge or maybe even evasion. Work written in the light of this, or in its shadow, has to be led by clarity, by precise description, by briskness of feeling, by no open displays of anything, least of all easy feeling; it implies an acceptance of what is known. The revelation comes from what is left out. The smallest word, or the holding of breath, can have a fierce, stony power.

This way of toning down expression happens most fruitfully in fragile places, or indeed in languages that are themselves under pressure. In the stories in James Joyce's *Dubliners*, for example, the tone of 'scrupulous meanness', as Joyce himself describes it, allows his characters to wander in a solitary place for the spirit as much as a real city. Also, the calm, precise style which Elizabeth Bishop used in her poems of Nova Scotia allows for a vast unspoken-of pain to emerge as though pushing its way through the gaps between the words.

These two artists, throughout a long exile, sought to be exact about feelings as much as places. When they allowed the tone of their work to soar, they had earned the right to do so by holding back so much in the pages which came before.

Bishop wrote, using this restrained style, about the life and longings of a young girl in poems such as 'In the Waiting Room', 'First Death in Nova Scotia' and 'The Moose', just as James Joyce wrote about the uncertain consciousness of young boys in the early stories in *Dubliners*.

Mercè Rodoreda, in her novel *The Time of the Doves*, written in Catalan and published in 1962, deals with innocence and inexperience, as Natalia, who works in a shop, takes in the world as though it might soon break on her, or disappear, as it indeed does, because of the Spanish Civil War. Natalia's consciousness is fully delicate, yet she maintains an astonishing ability to notice details, to render what is visible. The tone moves between the fully ordinary and the strangely incantatory.

Mercè Rodoreda was born in Barcelona in 1908. At the age of twenty, having received ecclesiastical permission, she married her mother's younger brother. They had one son. Between the early 1930s and the outbreak of the Spanish Civil War in 1936, she published several novels and pieces of short fiction, all in Catalan. In 1935 she began work for the Catalan Ministry of Information. Franco's victory in the war forced her to go into exile, first outside Paris but then, as a result of the Nazi occupation, elsewhere in France. Before she left Spain, she broke up with her first husband. After much difficulty and hardship, she finally settled in Geneva, returning to Catalonia in 1979 where she died four years later.

In her best fiction, she allows the details to speak for themselves; the mind through which the world is seen is almost naive, almost detached. This means that much is achieved or hinted at by tone, through rhythm, by coiled implication. The world is viewed as though helplessly, as if it might not bear the weight of much analysis. It is up to the reader to understand the extent of the suffering, the quality of the pain. The less these things are actively named, the more deeply they will be evoked.

If *The Time of the Doves* is a book of tender and subtle grace, filled with a deep innocence, *Death in Spring*, published in Catalan three years after Rodoreda's death, is a much darker book.

Rodoreda wrote from an exile more intense and lonely than that of Joyce or Bishop. She had not merely lost Catalonia, but she was writing in a time when the very language she wrote in – Catalan – was effectively banned by Franco, consigned to the private realm. She wrote her best novels at a time when they had little chance of finding many readers. She wrote in a language which was alert to silence, danger, fragility.

Death in Spring is like an ominous painting by Miró, made up of some essential elements – tree, lake, fire, mountain, wind, summer, winter, blood. Told through the consciousness of a boy soon to be a young man, it works through a mixture of simplicity and density of texture. Some of the sentences read like lines in a poem; others are replete with calm, casual, convincing detail.

If the book uses images from a nightmare, the dark dream is rooted in the real world, the world of a Catalan village with its customs and hierarchies and memory. But Rodoreda is more interested in unsettling the world than describing it or making it familiar. 'The village,' she writes, 'was born from the earth's terrible unrest.' She is concerned to dramatize that unrest using tones that are estranging, while also harnessing closely etched detail, thus creating the illusion that this place is both fully real and also part of an unwaking world of dream.

Writing one declarative sentence after another, setting down facts, explaining nothing, allowing the rhythm to become increasingly more urgent and the tone more disturbing, Rodoreda can create an atmosphere that is vivid and frightening. Rodoreda takes enormous risks as image after image of death and violence and grief are set down in a prose that is close to reportage but can also become soaringly beautiful, almost apocalyptic. ('In black night, standing in the moonlight on top of the stone clock, I was Time. The moon gazing at me. Time moved forward with difficulty, and as I stood there, something fled from within me, from the hour, from Time.')

The style is urgent, serious, unplayful; it shifts between the language of fact and the sound of prayer and then soars beyond the ordinary, as in the novels of László Krasznahorkai, to evoke panic and unrelenting dread.

Rodoreda's genius in this late masterpiece is to lure the reader's attention away from her terrain as merely emblematic or symbolic and make it seem lived-in, real, part of history rather than fantasy. This is a landscape of the soul; but it is also full of dark feelings and forebodings that are sharply present and ominous and persistent.

The fact that it was not published in the author's lifetime adds to the book's mystery. It was written in an exile not merely physical but also a place of spiritual alienation. Ths distance Rodoreda travelled between the carefully managed tones of *The Time of the Doves* and the uncompromising horror and dazzling complexities and energy of *Death in Spring* is one of the great journeys taken in twentieth-century fiction.

Colm Tóibín

Part One

I

I removed my clothes and dropped them at the foot of the hackberry tree, beside the madman's rock. Before entering the river, I stopped to observe the color left behind by the sky. The sun-dappled light was different now that spring had arrived, reborn after living beneath the earth and within branches. I lowered myself gently into the water, hardly daring to breathe, always with the fear that, as I entered the water world, the air – finally rid of my nuisance – would begin to rage and be transformed into furious wind, like the winter wind that nearly carried away houses, trees, and people. I had sought the broadest part of the river, a place farthest from the village, a place where no one ever came. I didn't want to be seen. With the mass of water descending from the mountains, snow and streams escaping the shadows through cleft rocks, the river flowed, confident of itself. All the waters joined together in the delirium of joining and flowed endlessly, land on both sides. As soon as I had passed the stables and the horse enclosure, I realized I was being followed by a bee, as well as by the stench of manure and the honey scent of blooming wisteria. The water was cold as I cut through it with my arms and kicked it with my feet; I stopped from time to time to drink some. The sun, filled with the desire to soar, was rising on the other side of Pedres Altes, streaking the white winter water. To trick the bee that was following me, I ducked under the water so it would lose me and not know what to do. I was familiar with the obstinate, seven-year-old bees that possessed a sense of understanding. The water was turbid, like a glass cloud that reminded me of the glass balls in the courtyards beneath the strong wisteria vines, the wisteria that over the years upwrenched houses.

The houses in the village were all rose-colored. We painted

3

them every spring and maybe for that reason the light was different. It captured the pink from the houses, the same way it took on the color of leaves and sun by the river. Shut inside in winter, we made horsetail paintbrushes with handles of wood and wire, and when we had finished them, we stored them in the shed in the Plaça and waited for good weather. Then all of us, men and boys, would set out for the cave on Maraldina in search of the red powder we needed for pink paint. The mountain was covered with heather and crowned by the dead tree, and the wind whistled through the brush. We climbed down to the cave along a knotted rope that had been fastened to a stake. The man who led the way carried a lamp. We lowered ourselves into the damp, black well; it was streaked with veins that would glisten in the sun, then slowly extinguish as we moved deeper and darkness fell, swallowing everything. Through the well we entered the cave, which was like the mouth of the infirm: red and damp. We filled our sacks with powder, tied them tight, and the men who stayed above hoisted them up and stacked them, one on top of the other. When we returned to the village, we would mix the crimson powder with water to make the pink paint that winter would erase. In spring – the blossoming, blooming wisteria draping the houses, bees buzzing – we painted. And suddenly the light was different.

We would leave in the dead of night with the wind always blowing on Maraldina mountain. The ascent was difficult. We entered the cave through the well and left loaded with sacks, one after the other, like ants. From the slope coming down the mountain, we could see the horses grazing, but they were used only for food. We cooked the horseflesh over a log fire, especially at a funeral Festa. At the slaughterhouse, the blood man was in charge of the others, all of whom were too old to do anything but slaughter horses, and the way the old men killed the animals made the meat taste of nothing, nothing but wood. When we climbed Maraldina, the harrying wind would push us backwards, and when we descended with sacks on our shoulders, the wind pushed us upwards. Whether going up or coming down, the wind beat against us as if it were pressing its huge hands against our chests. The old men explained that the low wind on Maraldina blew through the brush when no one was on the mountain. It carried souls that wandered the mountain with the sole purpose of creating fierce winds whenever we went in search of powder, rendering our work more arduous. The wind was telling us that ours was a senseless job, something that was better left undone. Souls have no mouths, so they spoke to us through the voice of the wind.

We would leave our sacks in the middle of the Plaça, and soon thereafter begin mixing the powder with water and painting everything rose-colored. All of the houses were pink except one: the house that belonged to Senyor. He lived at the top of the small mountain that was cleaved by a cliff and overlooked the village, protecting and menacing. The cliff, topped by Senyor's house, was covered with ivy that blazed in autumn and died soon after.

II

I craned my head out of the water. The light was stronger now, and I swam slowly, wanting to take my time before leaving the river. The water embraced me. It would have seized me if I had let it, and – pushed forward and sucked under – I would have ended up in the place where nothing is comprehended. Reeds grew in the river; the current bent them, and they let themselves be rocked by water that was carrying the force of sky, earth, and snow. I got out, the water dripping down my body, making my skin glisten. The bee that had followed me for a long time had finally lost track of me. I lay down on the grass, in the same spot where I had stood before, beside the madman's rock. A dip in the ground, that had been formed by a man hitting his head, had been turned by the rain into a bath for a black-crested bird. The dark shadow from the forest in front of me quivered. We called this grass *rosa de gos*, dog rose. Spiders were spinning webs from leaf to leaf, and insects – tiny, dead, dried – were trapped in threads that turned grey on cloudy days. I pulled up a clump of grass. Its roots were white and specks of dirt hung from them. On the tip of a curly root dangled an almost perfectly round speck. I clasped the grass by the blades and made it dance about, from side to side, but the dirt clung to the grass. I placed it on my knee as if I were planting it. It was cool. After a while, when I picked it up from my knee, it was warm, and I shook it hard to watch the dirt fall. Then I planted it again. In front of me lay the forest, where the elderly went from time to time, and when they did, they locked us chil-dren inside wooden cupboards in the kitchen. We could only breathe through the stars on the cupboard walls, empty stars, like windows in the shape of a star. Once I asked a boy from the nearby house if he was sometimes locked inside the kitchen cupboard, and

6

he said he was. I asked him if the door had two panels with an empty star on each side. He said, there's an empty star, but it's not large enough to allow much air in, and if the elders are long in returning, we start to feel ill, like we're suffocating. He said he watched through the star as the elderly people set off, and after that he could see only walls and ashes. Everything conveyed a sense of loneliness and sadness. Even the walls grew sad and old when the elderly left them alone and all the children were locked in cupboards like animals. And what he told me about things was true: alone, they grew old quickly, but in the company of people they grew old more slowly and in a different way; instead of becoming ugly, they became pretty. The elders would return early in the morning, yelling and singing in the streets, and sleep on the floor. Often they would forget to unlock the cupboards and the children became ill, their backs aching even more than when their parents beat them in a fit of anger. The village was painted pink, yet people still grew anxious because of the horses, because of the prisoner, because of the weather, because of the wisteria, because of the bees, because of Senyor who lived alone in the house on the ivy-covered cliff that on late summer afternoons looked like a wave of blood. And because of the *Caramens*, the shadows that crept among the shrubs, always threatening to attack the village. When a horse was born, the village held a Festa, but they didn't lock us in cupboards, nor did they lock us up during the Festa Major celebrations that began with the watchmen's dance and continued with people getting ahead of themselves in the race. They used to say that the day a man got ahead of himself, from then on he would have it easy, or mostly. Before dinner – after the dance and the race – a man, alone and naked, would enter the river and swim under the village to the other side, to ensure that the water had not dislodged any rocks, that the village was not about to be washed away. Sometimes the man emerged with his face ravaged, sometimes ripped away.

The ivy that crept up the cliff to Senyor's house died each year. The autumn wind stripped it naked, and all the courtyards were strewn with crimson leaves. This is the only thing Senyor gives us, they said, other than children when he was young. But not now. And they would laugh and look up at the windows. When all the ivy leaves had fallen, we boys collected them in our baskets and left them to dry; then we piled them up in the Plaça. When we burned them, we would look up because Senyor's head would appear through the long, narrow, middle window, and we would stick out our tongues at him. He would remain motionless, as if made of stone, and when the blue smoke disappeared, he would close his window, and that was it until the following year.

Senyor's eyrie was on the top of the mountain and the mountain was small. It looked like it had been split in two by an axe. No one ever went to the other side of the mountain. They built the village over the river, and when the snows melted, everyone was afraid the village would be washed away. That is why every year a man entered the water on the upper side and swam under the village and came out on the lower side. Sometimes dead. Sometimes without a face because it had been ripped away when the desperate water hurled him against the rocks that supported the village.

III

At night you could hear groans beneath the beds; the sounds were coming from the river, as if the earth were groaning, on the point of carrying everything away, as if everything would vanish with the water. But it didn't. The village remained, and only the water slipped secretly away. It was calm when it first arrived, but then turned wild with foam because it had dwelt so long in the dark. As though it had been frightened by being locked up for so long. I would sleep, and before falling asleep, or when I slept without sleeping, I used to think about things. I remembered my mother, without wanting to remember: straight and thin, with a red streak in her eyes. She used to beat children and spoil wedding nights. She would stand outside the newlyweds' window on their wedding night, howling like a dog until the sickly morning light finally silenced her. No one paid any attention to mother's howls, because she explained that her mother's mother had done the same, as did all the women on her side of the family. Like lightning, she would bolt out of the house as soon as the newlyweds closed themselves inside, and she would begin to yell and yell with her twisted mouth. When mother was dead and had been buried for some time, I – I alone – heard her crying out beneath my father's window the first day he and my stepmother slept together. It lasted until the first taste of light appeared.

One of my stepmother's arms was much shorter than the other. Before I fell asleep I would think about my stepmother's little arm, and I thought about the empty star in the cupboard where they locked me when they went to dance and laugh at funerals. I thought about the crimson powder and the cloud of souls and the tiny, reddish-purple heather that bloomed in autumn all across Maraldina. I thought about the sacks that bumped against the walls as we climbed out of the cave. The old men from the village, from the slaughterhouse, would come to the house when father was working in the fields. They brought things with them, and my stepmother would say to me: go help your father. And I would go, but when I would turn back to look at the house, it seemed to me that all around it wisteria roots were forcing it upward. I would walk along, kicking the dust, stopping at times to throw a stone at a lizard to cut off its tail, and then I would watch the tail trying to live, alone and desperate, until it became unbearable.

When I got out of the water I was fascinated by the sulphur dust that came from the marriage of flowers. A patch of it floated in a corner of the water. The sun was so strong that it made the blue round it less blue. Some sleeping fog broke up above the dog rose. When I had finished planting the grass, I thought again about Senyor's house. I could see the side of it, the side without windows. It was topped by a spire. I could see Senyor, in my thoughts, coughing and eating honey, waiting always for the river to carry away the village. The ivy, high on the rock, was green. From time to time two men with long canes would thrash the new sprouts that wanted to creep up the house. The shredded leaves would fall down the cliff, their tender blades and little hands uprooted, down, down to the roofs and courtyards. The ivy had to be cut back or it would devour the walls. Every time one of the men struck furiously with his cane, causing bits of leaves to fall, Senyor leaned out and looked down, his hands resting on the windowsill.

IV

I decided to stroll through the soft grass, up the incline; at the end of the slope the tree nursery appeared from behind some shrubs. The seedlings had tender trunks and no leaves; but after they were transplanted in the forest and grew tall, they would all carry death inside them. I walked among them, and they looked like objects you see only when you're asleep. I stopped at the entrance to the forest, at the divide between sun and shadow. I had seen the cloud of butterflies earlier. The trees in the forest were very tall, full of leaves – five-point leaves – and, just as the blacksmith had often told me, a plaque and a ring were attached to the foot of each tree. There were thousands of butterflies, all white. They fluttered about anxiously; many of them looked like half-opened flowers, the white slightly streaked with green. The leaves stirred and a splash of sun jumped from one to another; in between you could see speckles of blue. The ground was carpeted with old, dry leaves, and a rotten odor rose from beneath them. I picked up a leaf that was only a web of veins, like the wood and beams of a house, with nothing binding them together. I lay down under a tree and watched the cloud of butterflies bubble among the leaves. I looked at them through the web of leaf veins until I was tired, and as soon as I let it fall, I heard footsteps.

I jumped up and hid behind a shrub. The steps came closer. The shrub had a yellow, half-unsheathed flower and five leaves that gave off a prismatic sheen. The bee was sheltering there, dusting off its legs. I was sure it was the bee that had crossed the river and followed me from the village.

The steps stopped. Everything was quiet. As I strained to listen, I thought I could hear someone breathing. I felt a weight in the middle of my chest from listening: the same uneasy feeling I had when they locked me in the cupboard for hours, and the village was deserted, and I would wait. That was how I felt now. Nothing had changed: the leaves were the same, and the trees and butter-flies, and the sense that Time inside the shadow was dead. But everything had changed.

I heard the steps again, closer now, and saw a bright flash under the leaves. The man who was approaching carried an axe on his shoulder and a pitchfork in his hand. He was naked from the waist up, his forehead smashed. His face had been disfigured by the rushing river, and he was unable to shut his eyes because the skin on his forehead had healed poorly. His red, shrunken skin was pulled tight, always leaving a slit in his eyes. He had patches of black hair on his chest; his body was sunburned.

The bee seemed to be asleep, the flower too, until a gust of air arose and the flower swayed and the bee escaped from inside, graz-ing my cheek; and as soon as the flower was still again, the bee flew back in. The man left his axe and pitchfork at the foot of a tree, wiped his mouth with the back of his hand, and looked round as if he were lost. I was afraid he had seen me because his eyes stopped on the shrub. But he hadn't. He began moving from one tree to another, reading the plaques that hung from the rings. He tripped on a root and almost fell. Then he went deeper into the forest. When he was out of sight, I breathed deeply; the anxiety in my chest had kept me from breathing all that while. Flocks of clouds passed slowly by; I wished I could control them, sending them where I wanted. A cluster of very small ones came to a halt directly above the forest and stayed there a long time, giving the impression they did not want to leave. When the cluster of little clouds started to move away, the man returned. With his axe he began making a cross on a tree trunk; he had marked it with a stone, top to bottom and side to side. He worked mechanically, and after a while he dropped to his knees and began to cry. I held my breath. Still crying, he stood up, spit in his hands, and rubbed them together. The bee buzzed in and out of the flower. As the axe cut the trunk, you could see the line begin to emerge. With the first axe strokes, the butterflies went wild. Two of them flew down to the grass and stuck on one of the man's legs as he was cutting open the tree trunk. The bee was sucking the flower. The man rested and again spit in the palms of his hands. While he was rubbing his hands together, the axe under his arm, he looked up and seemed enthralled for a moment by the flutter of butterflies. He appeared more tired when he resumed work, as if each stroke of the axe bore all the weight of life.

Much later, the man began cutting the transverse line on the cross. One blow after another. The two butterflies caught on his leg were so close together, their wings folded up so tightly, that they looked like one butterfly. The man's back shone with sweat, his ribs too; he was very thin. I wanted to go over to him, speak to him, wanted to tell him that the blacksmith sometimes talked to me – between hammer blows, near the forge and sparks – about the forest and the dead people inside the trees.

The blacksmith had a house at the entrance to the village, a house with two wisteria vines, one on each side of the huge door, winding upward, covering the roof in a tangled mass of branches. As the sparks flew from the forge, the blacksmith told me: you too have your tree, your ring, and your plaque. I did it when you were born. When someone is born, I make their ring and plaque right away. Don't tell anyone I told you. All of us have our ring, our plaque, and our tree. And at the entrance to the forest stand the pitchfork and the axe.

V

I wanted to tell him that two butterflies were stuck to his leg, but I stood still behind the shrub, shut my eyes so I wouldn't see, and tried not to think. I didn't open my eyes for a while, not until I could no longer hear the axe striking. The man finished the transverse line of the cross and, using the pitchfork as a lever, he was prying the bark from the tree. It was difficult. When he had separated the bark, he grabbed one of the four ends with all his might and yanked it upward. He folded it back and nailed it to the tree with a large nail, using the back of the axe as a hammer. One after the other he nailed the ends – the four parts folded into the center – through the middle of the cross, then to the bark, the second nail above, the other two below. The trunk looked like a splayed horse. The tree was as wide and as tall as a man, and I noticed the seedcase inside. It looked slightly green in the green light of the forest, the same color as the tree trunks in the nursery. The man poked the seedcase with the pitchfork, first on one side, then the other, until it fell to the ground. Smoke rose from the gap left in the tree. The man put down the pitchfork, wiped the sweat from his neck, and rolled the seedcase to the foot of another tree. Some leaves were caught on it. He knelt down, head bowed, hands open on his knees, not moving. Then he sat on the ground and looked in the direction of the setting sun, at the butterflies.

Many of the leaves on the lower branches were partially eaten away, others merely pierced by little holes. The caterpillars never stopped chewing as they prepared to become butterflies. The man looked up with eyes he could not completely close. The air became wind. The man turned round, picked up the iron plaque, and looked at it as if he had never seen it before. He rubbed a finger over it, following the letters, one by one, until finally he stood up, seized the pitchfork and axe and headed toward the entrance to the forest, the axe on his shoulder flashing from time to time among the low-lying leaves. He came back empty-handed; and as if everything were going to recommence, the bee returned and entered the flower and the man approached his tree. He was weeping. He stepped backwards into the tree. The two butterflies had disentangled themselves from his leg when he rolled the seedcase and were now circling together above some blades of grass. They entered the tree with him, but flew out before the final entombment and landed briefly on a tree knot before moving to the soft, rubbery seedcase, where they stayed. I had turned my head, and when I looked back at the tree, I saw only the cross and the four nails on the ground. The bee was buzzing furiously before my eyes, like a pouch with yellow and black stripes. Tiny.

I stood up, rubbing my eyes from the sulphur-laced dust, and walked to the foot of the tree. Everything was still, more so than by the shrub. Everything was calm: the flutter of butterflies, the living and dying of caterpillars, the resin bubbling up and down and side to side on the cross as it healed the tree's wound.

I was frightened. Frightened by the resin bubbling on its own, the ceiling of light hidden by leaves, and so many white wings flapping. I left, slowly at first, backing away, then I started to run, as if pursued by the man, the pitchfork, the axe. I stopped by the edge of the river and covered my ears with my open hands so I would not hear the quiet. I crossed the river again, swimming underwater because the bee was following me: I would have killed it if I could. I wanted it to be lost and alone in the dog roses where spiders lay in wait for it. On the other side of the river, I left behind the odor of caterpillar-gorged leaves and encountered the fragrance of wisteria and the stench of manure. Death in spring. I threw myself on the ground, on top of the pebbles, my heart drained of blood, my hands icy. I was fourteen years old, and the man who had entered the tree to die was my father.

VI

I passed by the stables and took the shortcut through the horse enclosure. Right away I heard the sound of hammering. In the last rays of sunlight, the village seemed to be wrapped in lilac-colored smoke. Bees were everywhere. I glanced at the slaughterhouse tower with its handless clock and the straggle of houses, some still standing, many leaning to the side from the weight of so much wisteria, so many jasmine vines. The sound of the river was louder once you left the village.

The blacksmith was short and wide with crooked legs. I had always liked going to see him: the hammer and anvil, sparks shooting from the forge, the iron screaming as if it were alive in the water. I had enjoyed these things since I was little, since the first day I had gone to see the blacksmith make rings, awls, plaques. The plaques for the villagers bore only their names. But a bee flying into a bird's open beak was engraved above the names of the dead from Senyor's household. They used to say Senyor was the last of his race. And then they would laugh.

At noon, especially in the summertime when it is hard to breathe and the shade is blue, the whole village echoed with the hammer striking the anvil. The blacksmith would say to me: You see? Medals with names on them. You see? Rings. Don't tell anyone I told you. When you were born I made your ring and plaque right away, and we went with your father to nail it to your tree . . . He talked to me about the forest of the dead; he told me he never went there until he became a man.

As soon as he saw me at the entrance, he stopped hammering. He had tangled hair, thick eyebrows, and large hands with stubby fingers, his nails cut short. A drop of sweat trickled down his cheek. I walked over to him and explained what I had seen. He didn't say a word. Instead, he plunged his head in the bucket used for cooling iron, put on some kind of shirt, and hurried out without buttoning it all the way up. I stood at the doorway, my teeth clattering. The blacksmith darted in and out of houses. A few frightened women called to their children. The blacksmith's wife emerged and pushed me away before leaving with the other women. Soon, along the part of the street I could see, men were running as if they were being chased. An old man from the slaughterhouse, his arms dangling awkwardly, ashen like all the old men from the slaughterhouse, walked by me and asked what had happened; before I could answer, a man told him that everyone was heading to the Plaça. I kept staring at the wall on the other side of the street. It was made of large rocks all fitted together, with moss in the crevices. The wall was very old, its grey and yellow rocks timeworn; when the long-bladed grass growing on it became too thick, the blacksmith would climb on a box and pull it up. I saw a clumsy human figure etched on the wall that day. The legs, which appeared to be swimming, rested on a yellow rock and the stiff upper body on a thin grey strip of rock. The partially-erased arms were raised. It had no face. Shortly thereafter, as I searched for the face, I heard people approaching. A crowd of men passed by, led by the blacksmith. The old man from the slaughterhouse who asked what was happening walked beside him, talking constantly. Old men were followed by young men. One of them, a very tall, thin man, was calling out to see if the cement man – who wasn't anywhere around – had been informed, offering to notify him and help with the mortar trough and trowel. They carried torches. The women passed me; the blacksmith's wife with the purple mark on her cheek walked between two older women, giving the impression that she wasn't looking. They marched right by me, in front of the wall. Pregnant women were last, behind everyone, their heads up, holding hands.

When they disappeared, I entered the nearest house. The door was open. Wisteria blossoms showered the courtyard; the bees no longer grumbled. I walked over to the star on the cupboard in the kitchen and glimpsed a pair of eyes observing me sadly, like an animal's. I returned to the street. The village seemed dead, like Sunday afternoons when people set out to look at the prisoner. The only sound arose from the river. I headed for the path everyone had taken, the straight path, the path with the dandelions you blow apart with a puff, the path with lizards whose tails grow back. The path beyond the slope that was full of dust in summer and mud in winter. When I reached the Pont de Fusta, I stopped on the bridge to look at the water that was filled with a kind of sky that was not quite a night sky. I scrutinized it with such fascination that I didn't realize the moon was shining until a cloud hid it.

Beyond the Pont de Fusta, the path descended. When I was little the path would pull me along as if I were suddenly empty. A cliff frightens you, stops you, but a slope is silent and sweeps you away. On a slope, man met shadow and they never parted. They established the village. The man, the shadow by his side, planted the first wisteria. But that's not exactly how it was. A long time ago when the oldest of the old men in the village was young, he witnessed the birth of everything. The village was born from the earth's terrible unrest. The mountain was cleaved and it collapsed into the river, scattering the water through the fields. But the river wanted to flow with all of its water gathered together and began burrowing beneath the crumpled mountain, emptying it little by little. The river never rested until all the water could flow happily together again, although at times it grew furious when it hit the rock ceiling. They say that one night, not at the bottom of the slope, but on the ground, on the rocks hurled from the cliff, the moon showed two shadows joined at the mouth. And it rained blood. That is how it all began.

A great storm arose. The thunder, lightning, and rain lasted all night.

VII

After I had left behind the Pont de Fusta and slope, I began to run. I stopped at the edge of the forest, out of breath. No sound issued from the forest, as if it had been swallowed up. I followed the line of trees until I arrived at the seedlings and entered the forest in the same place as before. Everyone was grouped round the tree, the cross bubbling, creating a border. The glowing torches turned the green of the low-hanging leaves a strange green. The butterflies must have been asleep because I could not see them in the high branches.

The blacksmith broke away from the crowd and approached the tree. My stepmother must have gone for the axe, because she handed it to him. His short arms were poised in the air, then he delivered the first blow to the vertical line marked by the cross. No one breathed. A woman, her arms extended, started to shriek like an animal and was led away to the river where she suddenly became quiet. A man stood beside me, on a spot where the torches shed only a faint light. I didn't know him; I didn't think I had ever seen him before. He turned his head toward me, and when he turned I could see his eyes, large and shiny. One of the torch bearers had moved, and I glimpsed the eyes of the man who was standing so close to me. The person who moved was at a distance, but the torch had cast the beam in the man's eyes. The man cupped his hand in front of his lips, speaking to me out of the side of his mouth, so no one would hear – he told me that he enjoyed watching people die. When he wheeled round to see what was happening, I stepped back further into the shadow. As the blacksmith was preparing to swing the axe a second time, the old man who had walked beside him seized him by the arm, and he told the blacksmith that the tree should not be opened with an axe – it had already been breached – and the axe blows could kill whoever was inside, if he was still alive. Then the blacksmith sent for a large branch and, with some help, shoved it as best he could into the tree, through the middle of the cross. Carefully, through the hole made by the branch, he pulled, cut, and unsealed the tree. Four men grasped each end of the bark and yanked furiously. The blacksmith spun round, his face worn and pasty, and announced that the tree was resisting; it didn't want the dead person that belonged to it removed. His mouth a square hole, his eyes glassy, my father appeared to be watching. The tips of his fingers were embedded in the sides of the trunk, and I am not sure if I saw it . . . his hair drawn upwards by the tree's colorless blood. The branch that had been wedged inside the tree was pinning him backwards, piercing his stomach.

They started to shout. They shouted at my father who had little remaining breath and was clearly near his end. He was still alive, but only his own death kept him alive. They dragged him from the tree, laid him on the ground, and began beating him. The last blows made no sound. Don't kill him, shouted the cement man. The mortar trough, filled with rose-colored cement, lay at his feet. Don't kill him before he has been filled. They pried his mouth partially open, and the cement man began to fill it. First with watery cement so it would slide far down inside him, then with thick cement. When he was well cemented, they stood him up and put him back inside the tree. They replaced the cross and left to prepare the Festa.

I stayed on alone; the tree was barely visible without the torches. I went up to it and placed my ear against the bark. It seemed empty. I looked up because I wanted to see a little starlight. As I gazed upward, I could feel my link with life snapping. I felt detached from everything. I searched for my tree; night was a hand, wrenching me from my father's tree, leading me to mine. I knelt down and crawled on my knees from one trunk to another, fingering the names of the living and the dead. I could smell the fretted leaves and trampled grass. When I lifted a plaque, the ring sometimes squealed, as if it were tearing something that was deeply hidden, something that thrust blades of grass and leaves on branches upward. A ray of moonlight helped me locate my tree; it was directly in front of my father's. The plaque smelled of rust. I would end my days locked in that tree, my mouth full of cement that had been mixed with crimson powder, my entire soul within. Because, you see, the blacksmith used to say that with the last breath, without anyone realizing, your soul flees. And no one knows where it goes.

The village was deserted. Only the grieving sound of the hidden river reached me. From time to time a blossom fell from the cluster above, grazing my cheek. This was the hour that roots strained to upwrench houses. When a large crack appeared in a wall, it was filled with cement and the house became safe again. I followed all the villagers, as though I wasn't following them. I could still hear the voice of the man in the forest. I entered many kitchens where eyes waited behind stars in cupboards, just as mine had waited for the elderly to come and free me. I opened the doors to all the cupboards, and the sleepy children staggered out. I made my way to the blacksmith's house, where I struck the anvil two or three times with my open hand. I walked further inside. The blacksmith's son was skeleton-thin, and they always kept him in bed. I went over to gaze at him and touched him, but he didn't move. I continued on to my house and went upstairs; I could see the glow of the fires on the other side of the stables, on the Festa esplanade. All of a sudden I wanted to go and see them. No one was home, and as I was leaving I ran my hand along the windowsill. No flowerpot stood at the window; my stepmother always had a pot with a flower on the sill. Sometimes the flower was white, sometimes red. But there was no flowerpot that day. My stepmother wasn't at home. She was sixteen years old.

The horses ate the juiciest grass, gorged on the sweetest alfalfa, chewed the flattest carob beans. Horseflesh, they told us, would replenish your blood. We ate it in a variety of ways: often raw (chopped up and mixed with herbs), roasted in drippings in winter, sometimes cooked over a log fire – always cooked over wood at funeral feasts. The fat was made into balls and hung from the ceiling in the kitchen or dining room. The balls of fat went well with the soap bubbles from the wash area where the water was playful; some hung from the courtyard arbors all spring, even part of summer. As though they were made of glass. The ones the children made almost always burst when shot from canes; no one could explain why some lasted a long time, others only a moment. If one ever turned into glass, we placed it carefully in the fork of the wisteria vines. At home, we had always had soap bubbles and balls of fat. Two or three times a week my stepmother would say to my father, go to the fields, I'm expecting some fat. And father would say, fine. I would also say, fine, very softly so they wouldn't hear me because the two of them were walking together and I was farther off. Then my stepmother would put the flowerpot on the windowsill, and that night she had a ball of fat hanging from the ceiling.

My stepmother was so short she had to climb up on a wooden box to put the flowerpot on the windowsill. While she was waiting for them to bring her some fat, she would drag the bed to the middle of the room, where she usually slept, and crawl into it. An earth-colored blanket lay across the bed. If father and I were at home, she would sit in a chair, her legs folded beneath her, head resting against the back of the chair. She would often sit like that when father and I straightened up the kitchen. Sometimes while sitting in her chair she would take a cane and rock the balls of fat with little nudges. Father used to say she thought only about playing. Some days he would fill a basket with wisteria blossoms and tell her, play. She would say she was working because she was stringing wisteria flowers together with a needle and thread, threading all the flowers through the stems. They were necklaces. Some nights she didn't want to go to sleep because she said she had slept all day, and on top of sleeping during the day, she couldn't sleep all night too. I would sneak down and watch her. I discovered she didn't want to go to bed because she wanted to eat the fat without anyone seeing her.

I slept upstairs. If I leaned out of the window, I had a glimpse of a speck of sky overhead. From my bed I could see the ivy wall on the cleft mountain. At times when I lay in bed, unable to sleep, I thought how I wanted to bring Senyor crashing down – especially in winter when it snowed – or help the roots upwrench houses, or walk the horses on Maraldina where no one had ever been. I would think about things like that with my eyes closed until I got sleepy. The last thing I would hear, while everyone rested with their eyes shut, was the river dislodging the rocks that supported the village.

I wanted to see the Festa, so I went. The villagers had gathered near the river, on the esplanade by the canes that whistled because it was windy. Tables and benches had been built from tree trunks. The horse hoof soup was already boiling in large cauldrons, and standing beside each pot was a woman who was removing scum with a ladle and throwing fat and lumps of cooked blood on the ground. For a funeral Festa, they killed horses and pregnant mares. First, they ate the soup, then the horse or mare, and then a morsel – but only a small piece because there wasn't much to go round – of the little ones the mares were carrying inside them. They made a paste with the brains; it helped digestion. They peeled them, boiled them in a pot used only for brains, cleaned them, and then chopped them to bits.

With one spoonful of the paste, you had plenty. It was mixed with honey and went down like oil, passing through your innards, leaving you feeling fresh. More than one spoonful and you went mad. Just one spoonful, they would say. The paste provided them with the stamina needed to raise horses, cut alfalfa, and trudge all the way to the carob trees to look for beans. They used to say that those carob trees had witnessed the birth of the village, the two conjoined shadows, and the first horse's leap as it neighed and emerged like a flame, all alone, from the middle of the river. They used to say that if those carob trees could talk . . .

I stood very still behind a clump of canes. They were still slitting open horses. They tied their legs and strung them up on a kind of clothesline; you could see the empty space inside them lighting up, glistening in the firelight. The blacksmith's wife – short and ugly, with the purple mark on her cheek – was peeling brains with the two women who had accompanied her to the forest of the dead. Suddenly she jumped up, telling everyone to be quiet. She thought she heard the prisoner neighing.

VIII

In the firelight the men and the women all looked alike. In the daytime they appeared quite different: some were tall, some short, some thin, some fat; some had more hair than others, or a broader or longer nose, or different-colored eyes. But in the firelight they all looked alike. In the very middle of the day, when they were calm and occupied, the only ones who looked alike were fathers and sons. Some sons were identical to their fathers; some, however, did not resemble them at all. This almost drove the fathers mad, but little by little they grew accustomed to the idea. They said it all came from looking. Near the canes where I was hiding, a group of dirty, disheveled women were sitting on the ground away from the fire, their eyes blindfolded. They were the pregnant ones. They covered their eyes because if they gazed at other men, the children they were carrying would also take a peek and begin to resemble the men. They said a woman fell in love with every man she saw, and the longer she was pregnant, the faster she fell in love. So, what with women falling in love and children looking, what shouldn't happen, happened.

They filled their plates with soup and sat down on the benches round the tables, like brothers and sisters, drinking the soup straight from their plates. The faceless men were seated at another table closer to the river; the men without noses, or their foreheads ripped away, or missing an ear, could sit at the table with everyone else and live like everybody. But the faceless men wished to be alone. They drank the soup with a funnel of sorts and chewed the meat with one hand grasping the hole in their mouths so the meat would not slip out. They were ashamed to live in the village and preferred to be alone. They lived together in an enclosure behind the stables and helped each other. Once a man had lost his face, he was always in the company of another faceless man. It was as though they had never had anything at all; being mutilated meant relinquishing whatever they possessed. They started work at night: they grazed horses, cleaned streets, chopped wood – all manner of jobs. When they were among themselves they talked about the water and the strange taste of the drink they were forced to swallow before swimming through the river. And the serpent, and the waterfall that sounded like it was hidden but was more formidable than Font de la Jonquilla, the buttercup fountain. They were always at peace, according to the elderly, because they had perceived truth up close. They were reborn, it seemed, after crossing the river; they were less driven and possessed greater clarity than before. But they died the same as others: one moment alive, then their mouths filled with cement, all the way down to their stomachs.

The canes whistled softly. When the villagers had eaten their fill, the shouts and cries of joy commenced. They called out to each other from table to table or ear to ear and laughed. The digestion-paste was passed round and all of them swallowed a spoonful. The blacksmith didn't want any, so they grabbed hold of him and stretched him out on top of the table. Two women pulled at his feet, trying to make him fall off, onto the ground. One was my stepmother. The pregnant women stood up to dance. They danced alone, giving the impression that each was planted in the ground. And they sang to themselves as they danced. They lowered their heads to their chests, raised them up, threw them back, and spun round as if they would be spinning round like that all their lives, amidst shadows and flames, without a man, alone, bellies protruding in front of them, hair unkempt.

Until the canes began to sway in the wind, I had not realized they had been still for a while. The sky had blackened, leaving no trace of the moon. The first drops fell, fat and far apart. If it had not been for the shouts, I would have heard the rain falling on the river. They sprang to their feet and started to run, pursued by the rain. My stepmother ran too; she was the last one I saw in the firelight. The smell of extinguished fires pervaded everything. The water fell on the dead coals, drenched ashes, gnawed bones and grimy tools. A flash of lightning drew everything out of the shadow, and suddenly everything died ... died ... filled with cement, upright inside the tree. Father was dead. I felt I could not leave him there, that I should go back. I crossed the river again at the Pont de Fusta in the torrential rain. At the end of the slope, I took the path that led to the forest of the dead. As I approached the tree, the rain stopped, and I could hear it making its way to the other side of the forest. The cross on the tree was bubbling; the tree was digesting. I rubbed a finger over the resin and pictured the wall with the people passing by, heard the voice of the man with shiny eyes and the screams of the woman who had to be removed ... and I had done nothing for my father. I gathered some resin and held it for a moment in my fingers. When it started to dry, I fashioned it into a ball and carried it for a long time in my pocket. My fingers were clasping the ball of resin the day the blacksmith told me things, and when I emerged from his house, I threw it away.

I left the forest by the seedlings and walked back toward the bridge, the Pont de Fusta, bordering the trees. A dead bee was trapped in a spider web suspended between two tall bushes. I broke the web and shoved it into the ground with the tip of my foot, bee and all.

27

Part Two

I

The birds always came from the direction of the cleft mountain. The ones in mourning were the first to arrive. They headed straight to the pasture where the horses grazed, cawing raucously and circling the sky all day long. On the following day they would approach the houses, raising an enormous din, soaring and diving as they hunted. The birds were black-plumed and black-billed; a white selvage circled their even blacker eyes. When they took flight, their tail and wing feathers would spread apart: you could almost count them. They would slowly take to the air, then suddenly begin making furious loops, their feet embedded in their bellies, out of sight, as if they had been misplaced. Straight away, they would begin building their nests in the forks of wisteria vines, where the entwined branches were most tangled. They made them with old grass they had scavenged from beneath tender grass, weaving the blades together with sedge that grew in the river. Once the nests were finished, they would return to the pasture and perch on the horses' haunches, running their beaks slowly through the dense horsehair. The horses were fond of the mourners and would stand very still, hardly breathing. They would live together for two full weeks. If anyone tried to approach the horses, the mourners attacked them with their beaks, and the horses would lower their heads and stomp the ground with their right front hooves. When the two weeks had passed, the birds would return to find their nests full of bees that had grown fat on wisteria juice, bees they quickly downed before laying three eggs. They would sit on the eggs a few days; then the white birds would arrive. These small, mateless birds had red eyes and short, wide tail feathers. As the white birds swooped down, the mourners would scrutinize them, then attack them furiously just before they reached the nests. But the mourners would soon tire, and the white birds would manage to lodge themselves beneath the mourners' feet and bellies and take over the nests, sitting on the eggs until the chicks hatched. Many were blood-spattered by the time they finished nesting on the eggs. If the white birds did not take possession of the nests quickly, the mourners would crush the eggs; and if the chicks had already hatched, the mourners would peck the little ones to death. The third of the mourners' three eggs held a white bird. No one knew its origin.

When the mourners were ousted from their nests, they would drift aimlessly above the water, through the canes, until the fledglings could fly. Then they would return to the village and kill all the white birds. This would happen at night, and on that night we scarcely slept. When we got up the next morning, we collected the dead birds, nailed one to each door, and threw the rest into the river. The newly-hatched white chicks fled; no one ever heard them or saw them fly. It was as though they had been transformed into leaves, settling among the ivy. I found a white bird once and hid it in some shrubs. When I returned a few days later, it had become a swarm of maggots that stuck to your hand.

The mourners remained in the village until the end of summer, and when everything had turned blonde they would fly down the river toward the marshes. For a while some would wander back, roosting for four or five days on the slaughterhouse tower at Pedres Baixes, coming and going. When none was left, the elderly allowed us to take the nests apart. We examined how they were built and gathered the feathers that were caught in the nests.

My stepmother had a little box full of white feathers, another of black feathers. Sometimes, when we were tired of making soap bubbles in the courtyard, she would climb onto the table and take down the box of black feathers with the hand on her tiny arm. With the hand on her other arm — the one that was like most people's — she would take out the feathers one by one, letting them drop from as high as she could. They were the mourners coming.

I would collect them and pile them up on the table. Then she would take the other box and cry, here come the white birds, and the white feathers would flutter down, twisting round and round, a little slower than the black ones. The villagers used to say my stepmother was a bit retarded, but I didn't think she was. We played with the feathers in the early autumn when no birds remained. In the courtyard beneath the bloom-less wisteria, a few odd flowers would still be blossoming, those that had not known how to bloom in time. Hidden among the leaves, they didn't have much color. At times a weary wind would expose them for a moment, as if ashamed of displaying them.

II

My stepmother was shorter than me; she came to just above my shoulder. Her hair was straight and black, her eyes vaguely green. The corner of her eyes fanned out into thin lines, the same lines she had on both sides of her forehead and round her mouth. Like a little old woman. She fretted on the days she had to put the flower-pot at the window, in front of the curtain, and the lines would grow deeper, slightly dark.

I liked looking at her toenails while we sat on the step in front of the house: they were well placed on her toes and looked like glass. Sometimes they were sun-dappled with all the colors that arch in the sky from mountain to mountain after the rain. Her hair was mottled too, though more subdued, not as many colors. And her small teeth. She would settle in a corner on the days she was happy, from time to time laughing a howl-like laughter that gave a glimpse of the roof of her open mouth and her lizard-thin tongue. Little lizard arm, little lizard tongue. Her dresses fell straight from the shoulder, trailing the ground. In winter her feet and hands turned purple. She said they hurt. She was always cold. It took her a long time to reach the window and leave the flower-pot on the sill because she could hardly walk.

She had a sweet tooth: she would rub her hands with sweet-smelling herbs before cupping them to drink from the fountain. I tried it, but the water always tasted the same. I caught her one day eating a bee. When she realized I was watching, she spit it out, saying the bee had flown into her mouth. But I knew she ate bees. She would choose the ones that had drunk the most wisteria juice and keep them alive in her mouth for a moment, let them play a little before swallowing. One day when we were walking along the stone path, I cut off a lizard's tail, and she threw a rock at me.

34

The lizard was stunned. She picked it up and tried to reattach the tail. Then she stared at me and put it down without uttering a word, giving it a shove so it would scurry away while the tail finished dying.

Not much was known about her father. Her mother hanged herself. The old men at the slaughterhouse took her in, but when she had grown up a bit, she began following my father like a shadow. Father finally brought her home with him. She would fall asleep on top of the table, and father would pick her up in his arms and carry her to bed. Some nights I would reflect on things and sneak down to listen to them sleeping. I would steal down the stairs, keeping close to the wall because one of the steps creaked. Standing in front of their room, I would imagine she wasn't sleeping with father. I would imagine she was sleeping alone, and I was afraid she was choking, choking on a bee inside her mouth, between her cheek and gum. Maybe it was flying round inside, waiting for her to fall asleep so it could escape to the courtyard with its last remaining breath. She was wild about horse fat. She would climb up on the table to take down the balls of fat she had been given. She would scoop the center out, little by little, and when father wanted to eat one, he almost always found it half-empty. If he scolded her, she went off to her corner and laughed that strange laugh of hers. But the two of them walked together and I stood apart.

She didn't know how to swim. All the boys and girls in the village swam. But not her, because of her arm. She would sit on the riverbank and gaze at the water, sometimes plunging her feet in it, kicking and splashing water on her face and dress. When she was completely soaked, she would rub her face with both hands at the same time, then kick the water even more furiously. One day she wanted to go all the way into the water, near the canes, in the shallow water. The afternoon air was filled with color, and on the opposite bank everything had a slight tremor. Right away she wanted to go further into the river, but the water was already up to her waist. Then she slipped. I don't know how she did it, with that tiny arm of hers, but she grabbed hold of my ankle. I lifted her up and her lips were pale. We climbed out of the river, water dripping from her dress, and she headed home. I stood and watched her until she was just a black speck in front of the houses.

I jumped back into the river. The water that enveloped my legs still seemed to hold her. We had been in this water together. Mourners were flying above the blue and purple river, beneath the branches, searching for mosquitoes and soft grass. Night arrived, and suddenly I scarcely knew my way back to the village: from Pedres Baixes to the slaughterhouse and from the slaughterhouse to the Pont de Fusta, where the river beneath the bridge transported stars and pieces of moon.

III

The white flower was the same as the red: the only difference was color. Five little leaves, five larger ones beneath, and a handful of yellow threads crowned by a little saucer sprouting from the heart of the flower. They bloomed year-round. When one withered, a new one immediately shot up inside the dead flower: death thrusting life upward, summer and winter, endlessly. The only flowers like that in the whole village were my stepmother's. We didn't know where she found them. The day she entered our house, she set the two flowerpots on the table. Father brought her bundle of clothes; the bundle and the two flowerpots were all she possessed.

The first night we were by ourselves, I sat on the floor by her door. Inside she was alone and I thought I could hear her sleeping. I imagined her covers had fallen off, like when my blanket would slide off the bed and I couldn't be bothered to get up and put it back. While I was turning this over in my mind, I fell asleep. I woke up when I sensed I was being watched. Two eyes were bent over my face, two little rabbit eyes, small and round, like a shadow shining. When she realized I was watching her, she moved away, to her corner. The corner where she always retreated whenever father scolded her.

She would have stayed there if I hadn't told her to sit at the table with me. She came and sat, and I told her that her hair was mussed and she laughed, and when she laughed she seemed so tiny. Then I combed her hair. I made four braids for her – two in front, two in back – like the four corners of the earth. I tied a rope round her waist and right away the dress was shorter and didn't drag the floor so much. When she was all fixed up, we went out to the courtyard and collected wisteria blossoms to make necklaces. Then we lay flat on the ground to watch the roots emerging from the earth, lifting the house. We exposed the base of the largest

37

root and the deeper into the ground it went, the whiter it was, as white as the worm clinging to it.

I would have spent the whole day with her, but in mid-morning she told me to leave, she had work to do, and while she was telling me this, she was unraveling her braids and shaking out her hair, which again fell down, past the rope I had tied round her waist. I left, and when I was some distance away, I turned round: the window was open and she had placed the pot with the white flower on the sill; she was watering it. The curtain fluttered in the wind. When I was little, mother would take the curtain down to wash it and I would secretly breathe in its musty odor. When it was washed, it smelled of soap.

That afternoon I discovered my father wasn't my father. My fingers were firmly clasping the ball of resin in my pocket when the blacksmith told me he was my father; he said he would have to take care of me. He said all you had to do was look at my face, especially from the mouth up. He said he was my father, and that was why I always liked to keep him company, just like my mother, who couldn't walk by without stopping to look at the sparks and listen to the iron screaming in the water. He showed me a corner of the forge, where pieces of old iron and rusty chains lay, and told me that was where they had made me. I looked at his crooked legs, and when he noticed, he told me I had a bit of everyone. Then he laughed, and his teeth were drenched in saliva.

When I was little, mother was like a bee, buzzing from one place to another, kitchen, pasture, river, her braid black as night and teeth the color of bitter almond. When she raised her arms to hang clothes in the bright sun, it was as if the morning light was rising. She spoiled wedding nights because all the women on her side of the family had done the same. Like shadows that possessed a voice. The voice from those shadows screamed and screamed through her mouth all night long beneath the newlyweds' window. Then my mother grew ugly. Her eyes became sad; her braid lost its luster. And her cheeks. And her shapely arm. Her elbow no longer seemed pretty or made of honey.

IV

Font de la Jonquilla, the buttercup fountain, dried up that summer. The old men from the slaughterhouse talked about it in the Plaça; they said it had never happened before. The river ran only half as high as usual. Beyond the bend, past the tree cemetery, you could see the sandy bottom in places. The flowing water was earth-colored. Horses would go into the river, many of them rolling in it all day. People were afraid the village would sink. They said the drought was worse than the water from the melting snow coursing beneath the desperate village. Everything looked burnt: grass, ivy, wisteria. Courtyards were full of dead bees. Grey, white-bellied snakes from Pedres Baixes slithered into corners. They hid wherever they could, as a nursing mother realized one morning when she found one attached to each breast. They killed the snakes by beating them with canes and stones. The Muntanyes Morades were quite far away, yet seemed so near. They changed colors — grey in winter, blue in spring — so we never knew their real color. Maraldina was different; it was dark green all year, and when the heather bloomed it had a reddish-purple streak. The flatland from the river to Pedres Baixes was riven with cracks that slowly widened, forming a colorless, butterfly-like design. Night was suffocating: the hot shadow settled on your chest, giving the impression it wanted to crush you. I saw stars falling on the other side of Maraldina, beyond the forest of the dead.

One night, perhaps the brightest of all — sky taut, moon low — I heard the front door open. From the window I saw my stepmother strolling up the street. I went down and followed her from a distance. Doors were closed, windows open, the pebbles on the pavement beneath my feet hot. I felt someone staring at me from behind a window. It caused me more anguish than the anguish caused by the sleeping people. Not a single leaf stirred. When I had left the village behind, I found the earth warmer than the pavement. My stepmother had a strange gait. When I finally realized she was stepping from crack to crack, I became afraid she might get caught in one, like a fox in a snare. She stopped, and so did I. We seemed little because everything was very large and very dead. Legs helped draw us near other people; without legs everything would be isolated. I was thinking about legs because fear had settled there. My stepmother started walking again, heading for the Pont de Fusta. When she reached it, I sensed she had seen me, and I wanted to draw near. She was standing in the middle of the bridge. Just the thought that she was waiting for me set my hands sweating, and I rubbed them on my clothes. As I approached, I started thinking things I had thought before: people are closed in, but they open up when you approach them. Instinctively I opened my mouth wide and shut it slowly because an open mouth courts fear. I wasn't sure what she wanted. I stopped in the middle of the bridge and leaned over to gaze at the water, not thinking, just listening. She leaned on the railing too, and we stood for a while watching the water flowing calmly. The stench of putrid fish rose from the parched river. The smell merged with a flash of lightning – a falling star – and her voice. She told me she had left the village because she preferred expansive heat to the narrow heat between walls, among houses. When she asked me whether I preferred day or night, my hands started to sweat again, and I rubbed my palms against the tree trunk that served as a railing; it was rough. I told her I didn't know, but when I was little, even though I was afraid of night, I liked it more than daytime because you could see things too clearly in the light, and the utter hopeless ugliness of some things became too enormous. I told her then that I had left the house because I had seen her leave, had followed her, and a man had watched me from behind a window, frightening me. She told me that fear was nothing, and had I noticed there were two types of fear? One real, the other pretend. She had suffered real fear, the fear of hands, because hands can grab you. My fear of the man who had watched from the window was pretend, because from inside he couldn't hurt me at all. She took a stone out of her pocket and threw it in the river. I asked her if she too had noticed the odor from the river, but she said she didn't smell anything; one day we would go to the Pont del Pescador because the thing she most liked about the village was the bridges. I told her during fishing season the Pont del Pescador drank so much fish blood that just the thought of it caused me anguish, and my father had often taken me fishing with him on the days when others went to stare at the prisoner. I told her I found it all strange: the two rows of men, one at each railing on the bridge. When they caught a fish, they jerked the cane up in the air very fast, removed the fish from the hook, and flung it on the ground. Sometimes the fish would be stunned; sometimes it would leap up and fall back in the river. To keep it from flopping about, they would crush the head with their heels – if they could – slowly, so the blood would ooze out the gills without splattering them. When the fish was dead, my father would make me throw it back in the water. I would walk home again beside my father, my hands open, not knowing what to do with them because they were covered in scales. She said she had never understood why they fished, hour after hour, glued to the railing on the bridge, only to throw the fish back in the river when they were dead. As she was speaking, we started walking again, falling silent for a moment, till we reached the end of the bridge. Then we ran all the way down the path. When we got to the fork – one side leading to the forest of the dead, the other to Maraldina – she told me she wanted to climb the mountain. We'd go down into the cave. But first she wanted to visit the cemetery below the heather, where people without souls were buried: those who died alone or from some misfortune. I told her I didn't want to go into the cave; I would walk with her only as far as the cemetery at the foot of Maraldina, no farther. She took my hand, and we climbed up to the first cluster of heather. She drew me along, so I would go with her. I pulled away, in an effort to stop; then she let go of my hand

and started up without a word. I called to her, told her we hadn't gone to the cemetery for people buried in the ground, and she turned round. She was still close by, and in the moonlight her face was white as a root. She said we'd go another day, she wanted to climb down the well because it was cool.

I began the ascent. The seemingly endless path snaked through the tall thicket. I spotted my stepmother's shadow, half-hidden at times by the heather. She grabbed hold of twigs to keep from falling. She stopped for a moment, then abruptly vanished. I turned round to look at the view: below I could see the shimmering river that separated two strips of darkness. Looming above everything stood the slaughterhouse tower, the side with the clock sphere shining in the moonlight. You could see a brighter patch, the stables, and two or three windows lit up. Senyor's house was silhouetted against the night. The wind whirled dust, and I was consumed by fear: fear of the village so quiet beneath me, its houses filled with sleepers. I spun round quickly, toward the mountain, and again caught a glimpse of my stepmother's shadow in an opening in the path. I could tell she was looking at me, so I lay on the ground to be out of sight. Dust blew into my eyes and mouth. When I stood up, the heather was moaning. As I walked along I could feel the sleepers weighing things down, digging. Again, fear returned to my legs, the fear of night, the memory of revisiting my father's tree. When this fear pierced me I always wanted to run away, but I couldn't. Fear kept me scurrying between my father's tree and the blacksmith's house.

The wind was tiring. I glanced up the mountain and caught sight of my stepmother at the foot of the dead tree. When I drew near, I asked her what she was doing. Embracing the trunk, her cheek against it, she said she was thinking about things, things about my father and her, and the moon gazing down at us. She stretched out her hand and stroked my brow three times with her finger. I felt the urge to embrace the trunk, and when I finally did, my cheek against it too, I placed my arms and cheek higher than hers and we didn't touch.

She let go and forced me to do the same. Again, she told me she wanted to climb inside the well, so we walked down the mountain a bit and stopped in front of the entrance. The access was steep, very steep, but some rocks served as steps. Had it been daytime, and if we held on to the rope, the descent would not have been difficult. A cool, damp air rose from the well. She made me go first, practically shoving me, and even though I stepped from rock to rock, my legs felt numb. Inside it grew darker and darker. When I reached the bottom I was stiff and felt like crying. I felt I would never again be able to leave the well; I would smother to death because the entrance would be closed off, or the rope would break . . . She descended slowly, blocking the little bit of sky I could see. She pushed me further inside, then clasped my hand again, telling me she had been afraid the first time, but she had killed the fear because it was bad for you. Her heart had almost run away. She made me sit down near her. I wanted to know where she was, and I stretched out my arm, groping for her left and right, but found nothing. Still sitting, I began edging backward until my shoulder hit the wall. I searched for my stepmother with my outstretched hand. Suddenly I let out a yell that echoed in my ears as if it had issued from someone else: she had dug her teeth into my hand. I shoved her away and with my other hand found a mound of dust. It was cool, and I sank my aching hand into it. I grew accustomed to the dark, even though I couldn't see a thing, just a thread of dying light spilling down the shaft. Soon, not even that glimmer reached me: the moon must have shifted. The fear within me began to subside, replaced by a sense of peace as I sat, head against the wall, eyes shut. Then she began to speak. In a thin voice she told me that her father had died swimming under the village; no one ever saw him emerge. Every day, at the same hour her husband had died, her mother would go into the courtyard and stand there, head between her hands, rocking back and forth, back and forth. She told me that the day before the hanging, her mother had got a splinter in her foot and couldn't remove it, so she had to hobble. She hanged herself during the night, with a rope tied in the fork of the wisteria vine. The first thing she saw the next morning when she went out to the courtyard was her mother's dangling feet, but she wasn't at all frightened. She didn't know then what a hanged person was, or that the position her mother was in meant she was dead. Using her two fingers as pliers, she had removed the splinter from her mother's foot. She told me she didn't really know where her tomb stood, but she was sure it was where they bury the soulless dead, at the foot of Maraldina, with no marker. That was why, on her visits to Maraldina, she was always afraid she would step on her mother. She said if she hadn't been hungry, she would have been fine the whole time she wandered through the village streets, even though she could hardly remember it. When the old men from the slaughterhouse took her in, they gave her a lot of blood to drink, and that was why she was so strong. One sunny, winter day she began to follow my father; his shadow, she said, was warm. She told me her feet were cold and asked if I wanted to warm them. I don't know how she was sitting, but she put her feet in my lap and I took hold of them. They were freezing and, as I held them, I must have fallen asleep.

V

On the way back she told me she didn't want to walk through the village. The faceless men would be sweeping the streets, drawing on the last bits of straggling darkness, and they frightened her. We headed toward Pedres Altes, through the fields of thirsting, fractured land. We sat down on top of the sundial. It was a round, flat stone the color of dry mud, black-flecked. The blacksmith told me the sundial used to stand in the middle of the Plaça; he had marked the hours and forged the pin in the center to signal them. A year later someone had stolen the pin, but no one cared; no one wanted time in their lives. From where we were sitting, we could see clumps of canes and a few birds flying low over the water. The sun came up, and we watched the sunrise, our eyes wide-open, though we wished they were closed. It was a globe of fire, splashes of flames everywhere, all of it ablaze. When we closed our eyes, a black spot quivered before us. We heard the hammer beginning to strike the anvil. She got up and stood right in the center of the stone, placing her feet firmly together to cover the hole where the iron pin had been. She said she would be Time. She stood very still, casting the edge of her shadow between two hours. Slowly, the shadow moved. Later, as the young men were leaving the village for the stables and the eldest for the slaughterhouse, her shadow rested on an hour before inching away. Once more it came to a halt between two hours. I asked her if she knew what time was, and she said, Time is me – and you. She made me stand beside her; I took her by the shoulders, and she took me by the waist. The sun dispatched a trail of misty haze over the slopes of Maraldina and Senyor's mountain. And while we were Time, a strange force arose within me, as though my guts had been made of iron, as though my mother, behind the forge, had moulded me from iron as she merged with the blacksmith. At that moment I understood what it meant to experience the force of the boy leaving childhood behind. She looked at me. I took her hand and made her step down from the stone; then she dropped my hand. I headed to the stables, she to the village. I turned back to look at her; she had turned round too.

From out of nowhere four or five children appeared, naked, with skinny legs and fat bellies. They yelled, go with the ugly girl, go with the ugly girl, and jumped up and down like goats. The oldest one threw a rock at me, and the others followed suit. Then all at once five or six more appeared from behind some shrubs and started hounding me with rocks. I couldn't respond to the aggression; there were too many of them. Besides, I was afraid that if I threw rocks at them, I would really hurt them. So I started running, and that excited them; they chased after me, their skinny bodies sunburned. I took the path to Maraldina, knowing that would tire them. They looked like little stumps, pursuing me, yelling, go with the ugly girl, the ugly girl. Without warning, a rock struck my upper arm and blood spurted out. Let's kill him, kill him . . . They continued to run, but I had gained ground. Two were boys I had set free from kitchen cupboards. When I reached the cemetery of the uncemented dead, they froze. I watched them; even from a distance I could see the fear in their faces. They stopped throwing rocks and were silent for a moment. The oldest boy, head up, straight as a staff, flung his arm forward from time to time, his hand open, yelling, go with the dead, the dead, and they all shouted, the dead. As they strode away, they swung their heads round to shout, the dead.

We returned to the cave that night. We left the house together and slept there. We cleared a space in the dust, and in our crimson bed sweet sleep enveloped the delicate skin over our eyes. My arm hurt. The blood had formed a scab. With a trace of daylight from the shaft, we made two beds, like two cradles, one beside the other, so we could sleep holding hands. We formed a mountain of dust for a pretend table, and mounds of dust for pretend chairs, and little piles of dust for pretend pots and pans and little cups and round platters.

Every night we would go to the cave. As soon as we woke up, she would tell me what she had seen while she slept. One night a finger of hers turned into a caterpillar, and the tip gave birth to a red butterfly that died almost immediately. Another night she saw bees forming crowns above the horses' heads, and the horses wore their crowns of bees. Then the bees crowned the old men's heads, and when the men slaughtered the horses, horses and men were crownèd by bees. On another night she saw a stack of horses' eyes, and the mourners swooped down, snatched them in their beaks, and flew away, high into the sky. When they could fly no higher, they let the eyes fall into the river, and the water carried them away, flowing past the wash area where the women exclaimed, look at the spangles floating in the river. They said the prisoner had hurled them. Then she explained why some soap bubbles turned to glass: the ones that quivered and rose little by little burst, but those that shot straight up did not.

Inside the well, we found another well. She discovered it. She said she could hear water beneath her and told me to listen. We held our breath. You could hear water flowing, just like I could hear the river from my bed. We stood up but heard nothing; we could only hear it if we were lying down. Stretched out on the ground, she began running her hand across the wall, very slowly. She located an opening in a corner, a long way from where we collected the red powder, and managed to squeeze through it. She crawled inside and returned much later, backing out of the hole. She said she had found a well with light and water flowing through it. The following day, I enlarged the hole with a shovel; every day, bit by bit, I widened it, until we could both go together to see the well and listen to the water.

We would throw red powder in our newly-discovered well and then go down to watch the river: we didn't know where the water flowing deep inside the well came from or where it was going. We scrutinized the river, searching for a thread of rose-colored water. But the water from the second well dwelt in darkness, and the red powder we threw in it . . . who knows where it ended up? We threw almost all the powder into the water, all we had piled up when we had enlarged the opening, all that slowly fell from the cave walls from one year to the next, the powder used for painting the village.

We didn't play in the afternoons. She stayed at home and placed the flowerpot on the windowsill. When the heat grew less poisonous, but still persisted, I took her to the forest of the dead. For a while we strolled from tree to tree, reading the names on the plaques. We found a low fence of thorny branches; the trees on the other side were very old, and on all the plaques, above the names, you could spot a bee flying into a bird's open beak. We made piles of dry leaves, the ones the wind had left from the previous spring, naked, just veins and nerves.

VI

In the autumn we resumed sleeping in the house; I slept outside her door. If I had trouble falling asleep, from deep inside the cloud that always dwelt within me would loom the unease – of night, faded summer, fled mourners, bees that had transported so much honey . . . the season that had banished the lingering light and green grass.

One afternoon, returning from the stables with a group of boys, we heard screams. A man thrashing ivy with a cane had fallen, landing face-down in the center of a courtyard, his arm extended. His fall had shattered the ravel of twisted wisteria. They were shouting because he was already dead, and they were still shouting when Senyor arrived in a carriage that was drawn by two grey horses, a crimson-colored glass lamp affixed to each side. The stout, aged driver opened the door and helped Senyor out. I had never been that near him. His twisted legs made it difficult for him to walk. A birth defect: he had come out wrong. The mid-wife who birthed him had grabbed him by the feet, yanking him out, twisting them. They left him like that, his bones forever contorted.

Between them, two men picked up the crumpled man and placed him in the carriage. Everyone was grumbling because the dead man's soul had already escaped. Senyor tried to calm them, told them not to worry, he wasn't fully dead, his soul was still in his mouth. Senyor spoke slowly, in a soft voice, and while he was speaking he glanced about, never blinking. Some believed him because they wished to believe him; others didn't. One said it would be better to tear down all the ivy, so they would never have to thrash ivy again. A few said if they pulled it all down, the vil-lage would be doomed because the ivy kept the summer cool. It swallowed the sun's strongest rays, rays the naked rock could never absorb. Worse still, the rays would rebound onto the village, making it as hot as the blacksmith's forge. Senyor kept telling them not to worry. He studied my face for a long time before climbing back into the carriage, where the dead man lay doubled up on the seat. The driver slammed the door with a dry bang, and the carriage pulled away. Bouncing over the round stones, it appeared to be on the verge of falling apart. The pregnant women had removed the bandages from their eyes, to look at Senyor when he descended from the carriage, and when their husbands realized this, they slapped them hard: first one cheek, then the other, one side, then the other. Slap after slap.

For a long time the village talked about the man who had fallen. He had plunged straight down, they said. The cane had slipped from his hand, tumbling down alone, slower than the man, until finally it lodged in the ivy. They talked until the first storm appeared. The horses neighed and tossed their heads, their eyes entranced, fixed, as if glued to a piece of wood. The river coursed by the village, laden with dead branches and leaves from Muntanyes Morades. My stepmother and I went to look at it. Powdery, star-shaped snow fell, and the water near the riverbanks froze. We tramped through snow that squeaked when it turned icy. We moulded mountains with the snow. One day we built a huge snow tree and bored holes in it; we looked at each other through the holes as though we were strangers, and then we laughed. The laugh rippled through the openings and crept into the spiral of our ears and continued for some time, before finally dying deep within our heads. During the snow season, we returned to the forest of the dead.

We came to a halt as soon as we entered: we had never seen it curded with snow. We had gone through the funeral entrance and stood there, holding hands, close to the axe and pitchfork. The trees were white, top to bottom. The trunks wore scabs of snow and ice that a dying ray of sunlight transformed into colors. From the highest branches hung glass twigs, glass stars and threads. The snow had turned to glass, glowing green and blue; a rose color filled our eyes until they almost died. We stayed until we sensed that we too were metamorphosing into trees. We could feel the frost-cold roots being born beneath our feet, growing, binding us to the ground. In the snow our feet were hard to lift; they felt lifeless. Before we crossed the bridge, we looked back, and all the forest was a forest of calm. From time to time snow tumbled from a branch, as though the branch had just taken a deep breath.

VII

Senyor's grey, hoary house, blotched by damp, had two spans of snow on the roof. The snow fell thick and constant. At the approach of darkness, it was shoveled into piles in the middle of the streets. On windy nights shutters on the windows banged open and shut; the wind screeched and soughed, making everything seem alive. Perhaps that winter the river would carry away the village . . . but winter was ending and the river was now melted snow.

It was time to go in search of red powder. The wind on Maraldina was like no other. Unremitting, never sporadic, it was a weary wind, furious to be compelled to storm through the heather, endlessly. As we scaled the mountain, the wind would wrench shrubs out of the ground, tossing them in the air where they remained for a moment mottled against the light. The shouts commenced as soon as the first men descended into the cave. There was virtually no powder. One man exclaimed that it was pointless to shout, shouting made souls happy. The man beside him announced that the souls weren't at fault, if such things as souls existed; what had happened was clear: because of the terrible summer heat, powder hadn't fallen from the walls. The man who said it was pointless to shout told them to be quiet. They didn't know what they were saying. The souls of all the unnamed dead were laughing because the villagers were shouting. He could hear them laughing.

The following day we returned to the cave with hoes and shovels to scrape the powder from the walls and ceiling. Breathing inside the cave was impossible. We emerged from its entrails red as rage. But the village had to be painted. Unpainted, from a distance it looked like a straggle of houses that were on the verge of collapsing – poor and begrimed, prisoners of the still dry wisteria. When I entered the dining room after the third visit to the cave, I found my stepmother sitting on top of the table, her head bent backward. Surrounded by paintbrushes, she was running a brush over her neck, slowly, as if she were painting a wall. As soon as she saw me, she stopped and said, now that it's dark, let's toss the brushes in the river. We wrapped them in a sack and set out to throw them away, hurling them as far as we could. We lingered, gazing at the black water, and had to hurry back because the face-less men that frightened her were beginning to emerge. The next day we searched for more brushes. They were stored in a shed in the Plaça. We didn't rest until we had got rid of them all. On the last day, it was still early so we went and sat on the sundial; we could hear the wind howling from there. She said we weren't hearing wind, but grieving souls.

When the wisteria first began to bloom, fresh grass sprouting, we returned to the forest by way of the river. To cross it, she clasped me by the waist, and I swam with her behind me, as though I were bearing a lily leaf. We were thirsty and swallowed mouthfuls of water, all the broad river wanted inside us. We left behind the dog roses and seedlings and sat beneath the black-smith's tree. All at once, I stood up and carved a cross on the trunk with my fingernail. We looked at each other and laughed. She picked up the plaque and held it in her hand for a long time, then spit on it to blacken it. I removed the ring and fastened it to another tree. She laughed and clenched her teeth, her tiny teeth, top against bottom. We stood up and began examining the trees; some were very old and the trunks were full of knots. We started to run. Racing through the forest like wafting leaves, we got separated. I called to her with a whistle I had invented, one she had learnt right away. One of my whistles enticed a shiny, black snake out from beneath a rock, and I picked up the rock where it had settled and threw it, killing the snake.

Everything pressed on toward summer, toward greenness locked deep in the forest. And we switched all the rings. Clusters of trees bore no rings at all; others had three or four. We scrambled over the thorny fence and studied the plaques with the bee and bird. Those were the oldest trees of all, their trunks all splintered. The tallest tree was full of dead branches, and when we removed the ring, mouldy moss dust fell, revealing a long hole from which a bone protruded. I pulled on it and more bones tumbled out, and she scattered them. Every time we removed a ring from a tree within the fence, a hole would emerge and yellow bones would spill out. I widened the holes and started pulling out the skulls: they were the bones that couldn't get out by themselves. We stacked them up, one on top of the other, and plugged the eye sockets with grass so they would not stare at us. The tiny bones from feet and hands were just right for playing. We would toss them in the air and catch them, and if one fell on the ground, the person who had let it drop lost. We had a hidden corner in the forest, imbued with the smell of moss, where we kept a stone that served as a pot, and we put lots of the small foot and hand bones in it. If we didn't feel like playing, we would go to the stone and stir the bones, hold them up, then let them drop, just to hear the little noise they made when they landed.

One day I wanted to hack open a tree with an axe; she stared at me with big eyes, her hand in front of her mouth. My right palm stung, but she was watching me and I didn't complain, hardly noticing the pain. The trunk was like rubber, and the dead person inside still had skin, grey as Senyor's house, stuck to the bones. Four snakes were slithering between the ribs, just like the one that emerged when I whistled, only smaller.

As the weather turned warmer, butterflies were everywhere. Sometimes we would throw a bone at some leaves and the butterflies would take wing, scattering. We lay down on the ground to look at them, and I fell asleep until I sensed I was being watched. She was kneeling in front of me, the axe in her hand. Slowly she walked over to a tree, turning back from time to time to see if I was following. I followed, and she stopped in front of the tree and, handing me the axe, told me to open it. A ray of sunlight trickled down between the leaves onto her hair, charging it with colors. Little flecks of color glistened like water in the white of her eyes. Open it. She handed me the axe, but I didn't take it. I looked only at her, and I could see her standing so close to me, yet only a short time before so far away: in the courtyard making soap bubbles, stringing together wisteria blossoms with a needle and thread, sitting on top of the table with a cane in her hand . . . standing in the middle of the window with the green curtain. Open. I didn't utter a word, nor did I move. Abruptly, she dropped the axe and started spinning round me as if she were possessed, open, open, open. Again, she handed me the axe, but I didn't take it. She marched off to play with the rings, and I stood before the tree, my eyes fixed on the axe lying on the ground.

I hadn't budged. Barefoot and tiny, she returned, strolling through the trodden grass, down the narrow paths we had beaten during our frequent walks. She sauntered along, carrying a round bone in her hand, throwing it up, catching it. We played at being afraid. They're coming, she would exclaim. And we ran back and forth, our hearts filled with fearful blood because we didn't know who was coming, from what direction, if there were many of them, or if it was just the one conjured up by the fear our voices awakened in us. They're coming, they're coming. We hid behind tree trunks. We would stand very still for a moment, then suddenly thrust our heads out from the side of the tree, quickly hiding again, as if each of us represented 'they' for the other; we never knew who they were – they never arrived. When we emerged from behind the trunk and listened, there was nothing to be heard: only the breath of light and earth, and the air that dwelt on high.

Again, she picked up the axe and again handed it to me. She lifted it by the blade, offering me the handle. Open. She never took her eyes off mine, and I grasped the axe and began to unbar my father's tree, top to bottom, side to side. It was soft. Trees that held the dead inside were like rubber, hard to breach. When I had opened the cross, she told me to pull, and, with her help, I pulled as hard as I could. Then it all spilled out. Bark and rotted flesh. And a watery mixture: black sweat from the body. At eye level stood the decomposing heart, partially attached to the chest by four veins and, above it, the mouth sealed with rose-colored cement; deep within lay a damp smudge of brighter pink cement. The flayed knees were bent, the bones twisted. Further up, the face – rotted fruit, forehead stripped clean – seemed to be laughing. But the eyes were missing, burnt by the sap. I ran away. I could tell she hadn't moved. Then suddenly I heard her laugh. I swam across the river, never stopping until I reached the house. When I entered, I found her already sitting on top of the table, scooping out a ball of fat with her finger.

I dreamt my father's breath was burning me.

VIII

A woman died in childbirth, and when they went to bury her, they discovered the forest had been ravaged. The weather that afternoon was troubled. The sky was sulphurous, not a leaf stirred. The unrest that had commenced at the cave returned. Between young and old. For some time the young from the wash district had been saying that people should be left to die their own death. The old men from the slaughterhouse argued that everything should continue as before. The middle-aged men were inclined to side with the elders, except for a few that no one heeded. One elderly man lamented the sad affair of mixing bones and stuffing grass in eye-wells, it should never have happened. The blacksmith wasn't listening; he delivered the first axe blow to the tree they wished to open. The wedge slipped off the handle. He told them to stop quarreling and go look for a new, broader axe head, one that wasn't rusty. An old man moved away, muttering, leave the bones alone, they can harm us. A young boy said, we should just live our lives, peacefully, us the living, and stop thinking about souls. Have you ever seen one? A woman covered her ears, her face white as snow. The man who had been sent to fetch the wedge returned, and the blacksmith slipped it onto the handle, pounding it with a stone until again he had a strong axe. They said order had to be re-established in the forest before the village could be painted. For many days in a row they went to the forest, endeavoring to restore each ring to its tree, each skull to its own bones. The women sewed the crosses on with thick needles and horsetail hair, because the trees no longer produced the resin to seal them.

For days my stepmother and I didn't speak to each other. If her eyes met mine, we quickly turned our heads, as if an invisible hand were pulling us by the hair, forcing us to turn. Day and night, I had visions of the tree: the hoary, green bark with white streaks. The malodor was everywhere, that smell coming from within, from the heart of the trunk, from flesh blended with live wood. I heard a voice telling me it should not have occurred. The ashen face of that woman, and my father's empty eyes that saw how mine . . . Soon she came to the courtyard with the boxes of black and white feathers and asked me to play. She climbed onto the table and let the feathers flutter down; I caught them and placed them in heaps, each color in its own pile.

We began to amuse ourselves by hunting bees. And crushing them. She gathered honey and put it on the ground, just a drop. When the bees came to suck it, we would squash them. Sometimes, instead of squashing them, we would cover them with an upside-down glass, imprisoning them until they died. That first night, I could hear the bees, the ones that weren't trapped in honey, buzzing and knocking into the tin walls. On windy days, we noticed that the bees collected a tiny piece of gravel with their legs and flew with the added weight, so the wind would find it more difficult to toss them about. When the wind stopped, they immediately released the gravel. We discovered this one day when a bee flew past my stepmother and dropped a little piece on her forehead. The older bees would fly to the fountain for the buttercup tear; many died on the return, strained by the weight. The younger bees would collect the infants with their snouts – they had deposited them on a leaf while they worked – and carry them away to sleep. The bees couldn't comprehend what was happening; they would fly to the sundial and bury their dead all round it. They were so sad that year: instead of sucking wisteria, they headed to the fields and sucked bitter flowers. They couldn't be bothered to fly into the folds of our clothes or the ravel of our hair.

The water from Font de la Jonquilla had to be filtered. In the fountain little worms curled and uncurled, rapidly. If they entered a person's body, they burrowed through bones, veins, and skin in order to escape. As soon as they broke the surface, they died, because they could not live without water.

IX

When the work in the forest ended, it was time to paint the village. And there were no paintbrushes. My stepmother and I hid behind the blacksmith's house; from there we could hear the shouts. Hurriedly they made new brushes, but not enough; they had to be shared, passed round from person to person. The village could not be painted quickly, nor all at once.

When the painting was completed, the thick-clustered wisteria had already finished blooming. The day of the Festa, everyone was uneasy: about the souls, the powder, the welter of disorder in the forest, the bees buzzing nervously through the fields (they must have told each other they were dying off).

The women had decorated the streets. From one house to the other, from one side of the street to the other, they had strung lines, adorning them with scraps of old, brightly-colored clothes. The blacksmith took the prisoner some honey, and when he returned he announced that soon the neighing would begin, the prisoner's mouth was already horse-like. Mid-afternoon, the pregnant women began to dance in the center of the Plaça. From a courtyard, someone started hurling stones against the rock wall, trying to free the cane, wedged high in the ivy, that neither wind nor rain had been able to dislodge. You could see the cane and stones flying past. All of a sudden the cane quivered, then fell; for a moment it seemed that it would again be trapped, further down. But it wasn't. The person who had freed the cane appeared in the Plaça and started breaking it into bits, handing them to whoever wanted a piece. He was young and tanned. The pregnant women stopped their dancing and approached the boy who was distributing the scraps; they removed their blindfolds, pretending to want a bit of cane, but they had eyes only for the young men round them.

When the boy offered one of the women a piece of the cane, she grasped his hand before anyone realized and planted a kiss on his fingernail. The blacksmith standing beside me said the villagers would soon be busy killing desire. I did not know then what they did to kill desire, nor what it meant. The pregnant women began to dance again, but they could see nothing. Before they resumed dancing, their husbands had retied the bandages so tight that they pulled the skin on their foreheads.

My stepmother was sitting at the entrance to the house, a ball of fat in her lap. Everyone who passed by shouted things at her, but she kept eating, never glancing at them. But as soon as they had passed, she shook her finger at them. The pregnant women finished their dance, and all the men lined up to race. They ran with their eyes bulging, arms in front of them, chests forward. They gave the appearance of being disjointed. Their breath preceded them, and they followed it. Two very old men had already prepared the hollow tree trunk with the short sticks. All of the sticks had sharp pointed tips, except one, which ended in a fork. The man who drew the forked stick was forced to swim under the village. The faceless men, the noseless, the earless, all of them shut themselves in the stables so as not to dishearten the others. The one who drew the forked stick needed to be brave, brave as the sun. The hollow tree trunk with the sticks inside was painted pink, inside and out. It was repainted every year, just like the houses. The men and older boys had to run past the trunk and seize a stick. When a sharp stick was drawn, everyone was silent. When the forked stick was drawn, everyone burst out laughing and the children jumped up and down.

A boy who was not much older than me drew the stick. His face was like others', but his nose was straighter, his cheeks more delicate. When he glimpsed the tip of the stick, he turned pale with the pallor of fear, and everyone knew – even before seeing it – that he had chosen the forked stick. Always, always, the one who drew the forked stick turned pale.

The blacksmith and a group of men accompanied the boy to the upper edge of the village, where the water from the river thrust itself downward, toward darkness. The boy stripped, and they gave him a drink; while he drank, his eyes wandered from one man to the other. He took too long to dive into the water, and the men had to throw him in, alone and naked. I had gone to watch, my stepmother beside me, and when the boy plunged into the water, she pulled a piece of string from her pocket and began swinging it. A man noticed us, and he struck me on the chest with his fist, knocking me to the ground. All of the men raced to the lower edge of the village to watch for the boy. In the Plaça, three women were pounding and mixing together wisteria blossoms and bees in a wooden mortar: this was the ointment to dress the boy's wounds, re-sheathing the skin over his blood. Senyor observed it all from his towering window. He was waiting for the boy to emerge and announce that the village would soon be swept away by the river. He could see when a man entered the water and when he emerged. If the man was unconscious when he reappeared, the villagers would fish him out and carry him to the riverbank. As soon as the man had left the water, Senyor would close his window.

My chest hurt, and I headed for home. My stepmother followed me. We sat on the step in front of the house. I looked at her and she laughed, and all the while the water beneath the village was thrashing the boy against the rocks, mutilating him.

X

When they pulled the boy from the river, he was dead; they returned him to the river. Those who died in the water were returned to the water. The river carried them away and nothing was ever known of them again. But at night, at the spot where the bodies were thrown into the water, a shadow could be seen. Not every night. Not today or tomorrow, but on certain nights a shadow trembled. They said the shadow of the dead returned to the place where the man was born. They said that to die was to merge with the shadow. That summer, the shadow of the boy was clearly distinguishable. It was unmistakably him because he had been separated from one of his arms, and the shadow had but one arm. Struggling against the current, the shadow – which was only will, not body or voice – attempted to slip beneath the village. And as the shadow struggled, the prisoner neighed.

Only one prisoner remained in the village. Long ago, there had been another, and he had lived, they said, twice as long as most people did. The prisoners were thieves: the village only punished thieves, and they punished them by taking away their humanity. The blacksmith built the prisoner's cage. He made it small, just large enough for a person to sit in, but not lie down. The first prisoner had had a wooden cage; everyone recalled how he passed the time biting his nails until blood spurted from them. Then he would begin to sob. The wooden cage rotted before the prisoner had ceased to be a person, and they were forced to build a new one. The iron one, they said, would last a lifetime. In winter, the villagers placed logs around the cage, so the prisoner would not be cold. Everyone loved the prisoner. They took him food and water every day. He was kept below the wash area, and when the women gathered there, the mad ones would call out, neigh, neigh for us. Sometimes, when the prisoner was alone, he would attempt to neigh, but instead of a neigh, a kind of yowl would emerge, a strange voice. On Sundays, many villagers went with their children to see the prisoner. They would toss him morsels of meat, close to the bars, and he had to catch the scraps with his mouth. If he couldn't catch them, he had to pick them up from the ground with his teeth, like a horse eating grass. When no more meat could fit inside him, he would close his mouth and eyes, shutting the villagers out, and on the following day he would be punished. If it was summer the blacksmith would smear honey on him, and soon the prisoner became a fury of bees. Before honey could be smeared over his body, he would be seated in a bucket, his ankles and wrists tied with heavy rope to the bars of the cage.

The prisoner was so thin you could count his ribs, and his eyes had red streaks like my mother's. No one knew what he had stolen, but they all agreed that he had stolen. If it was winter, instead of smearing him with honey, they would force him to drink unfiltered water from Font de la Jonquilla. Worms would emerge through his skin, and as soon as they did, they died, because they could not live without water. The prisoner was wasted after that, drained of strength. He would recover very slowly and open his eyes, without looking. I saw him once, hands and ankles tied, his head leaning motionless against his shoulder, a swollen vein in his neck.

That summer as the shadow struggled, the prisoner neighed and the horses responded. The following day, the whole village gathered to watch the blacksmith remove the cage. They lifted it in the air and abandoned it on Senyor's mountain. When the prisoner realized he was no longer surrounded by iron bars, he began to neigh with all his remaining force, spreading his arms and legs wide. He remained in that position, as if still tied. He is no longer a person, the blacksmith announced. The skin on his wrists and ankles had lighter-colored stripes, as if the sun had

63

been unable to penetrate the rope that sometimes bound him. Two men stood him on his feet, and when they let go of him, he fell to the ground, again spreading his arms and legs. The blacksmith turned to face the group and announced once more that the prisoner was no longer human, but he would live longer than they would.

XI

Another summer ended. It was as though all the dead autumns were the same, with their relentless insistence on returning. Autumn was here again. Nailed to the rock wall, from the ground to the top of the cliff, autumn was a surge of fiery leaves that would be snatched away when the sulphur-bearing wind returned, grown old and icy. Leaves fell on the village streets and on the river that carried them away. Swirling in whirlpools, they drifted to the clock tower, as far as Pedres Altes. They tumbled down, still bearing the scent of their former, tender-green selves. The sickly stems that had held the leaves all summer were now devoid of water, and they thudded to the ground as well. The leaves were blown down and swept away. We waited for the last to drop so we could rake them into piles and set fire to them. The fire made them scream. They screamed in a low voice, whistled even lower, and rose in columns of blue smoke. The smell of burnt leaves pervaded houses and air. The air was filled with the cessation of being. If the leaves burned too slowly, we poked the pile with a cane, lifting one side so the flame could leap upward. Little by little, spring died in autumn, on the round stones in the Plaça. Soon the first, small rain would extinguish the last warmth and unpaint the houses. Everything pink faded, vanishing in black trickles. The village was a different village with no leaves and no color. A village of weary, decaying houses, clustered together above the water, embedded in Senyor's mountain.

One night when the horses were standing asleep in their enclosure and the village was dead, my stepmother and I went out. We strolled past the horse fence, my stepmother's dress down to her feet, her hair to her waist, her forehead capturing the nocturnal

65

dew. She told me she had seen the blacksmith's son sitting in front of his house, mere bones clothed in skin, his face all eyes. We held hands as we walked; then all at once we laughed because we had turned to gaze at the shadows stuck to our heels. We jumped backwards, treading on them. We turned to face the shadows and they stuck to the tips of our toes, and we trod on them. Suddenly my shadow was longer than hers, then hers longer than mine. I caught an unfamiliar scent. I couldn't say of what herb or what flower hidden within the earth, something that – before going to sleep – was preparing the scent it would offer at the conclusion of cold. We climbed up onto the fence and sat on the rail. She told me she knew many things: far away the river was flowing; the dead were asleep; trees that held a dead person likewise died a bit; cement inside a dead person took a long time to dry. She said we knew many things about the light, about everything that transpires as it goes round, returning to us – neither too fast nor too slowly, like our shadows cast on the sundial hours. The same, always the same, no beginning, no ending, never tiring. You and I grow tired. She stretched out her arm, searched for my face in the dark, and stroked my brow three times with her finger. She climbed down from the fence, wanted to play, to make ourselves into a ball. We sat on the ground, our knees against our chests, arms clasping knees. We played for a while, leaning first to one side, then the other. Let's stretch out, she said, and roll far away. The trampled grass allowed itself to be trampled as it played with us. And the horses slept.

When we tired, we got to our feet. She turned and met me, and we stood facing each other. Her eyes shone, and within the dark gleam cast by the ever-higher moon, I seemed to glimpse the swaying leaf of a cane, a tiny one. Without a word, we began to run, as if we were flying; we stopped when we reached the center of the bridge, our hearts pounding.

The smell of the water rose from the river below, as though the water itself lived in the air, coursing through its channels. The scent of moist flower, earth, and root reached us. The water that flowed in smelled the same as the water that flowed out. The same, always the same. We looked, straining to glimpse what could not be glimpsed. Behind us, the moon pinned our shadows to the ground, slowly casting them onto the river; it partially erased them, and joined them at the mouth. When the moon died, it carried away the shadows, still joined at the mouth, as if it had dragged them away by their feet.

We had a little girl, just like my wife. And my wife always said: she's just like me.

Part Three

I

The day my child turned four, I took her to Font de la Jonquilla. She didn't want to go. I went with my father to the fountain when I was my daughter's height, and I had never been back. I remembered it as a dark hollow in the shade. I knew that once you passed the slaughterhouse the path followed the river, and you could see the wash area and the prisoner's cage on the opposite bank. Midway, the sound of the falls reached you. If you looked back after walking a while, Senyor's mountain began to turn sideways. When you got to the Pont de Pedra, the ivy-shrouded cleft came into sight; opposite it, a slope with trees at the bottom and grassland at the top. Three paths led from the Pont de Pedra. One of them winded up the mountain. The wasteland round the bridge welcomed only stinging nettles and weeds, weeds that – if you boiled and swallowed the liquid – would bring up everything inside you. My child stopped near the bridge to gaze at the river. When we left the village the sun was asleep behind Pedres Altes, but now it had risen and was sweeping through the bend in the river, splashing the green leaves, turning them yellow. The trees bordering the river beyond the Pont de Pedra had changed a great deal: when I was little I could touch the lower leaves – I liked touching them because their underbelly was white – but now I could hardly reach them. Soon after crossing the bridge you could hear the waterfall. The path dipped, then gradually turned away from the river till it finally ended in front of a cluster of thick-trunked trees that surrounded a circle of rocks. The spring stood in the center; it was not dark, dappled sun danced on the ground, and the mountain loomed in the distance. When I was little I had been frightened by the worm-filled spring that always spewed water; it was something alive that I couldn't understand.

71

The rocks where the water gushed were covered by a dense climber with white-flecked blossoms; the water that collected at the fountain trickled off, down a canal adorned with blue buttercups. Taking hold of my child's hand, I remembered myself at her age, my fear, my father, the first day my wife showed me the child and told me to look at her, saying she's just like me (the midwife who birthed her wanted to show her to me, but I didn't want to look because of all that had happened). The child stood still, her hand in mine, gazing at the buttercups. Bees were drinking, buzzing round the rocks and canal. I picked a buttercup and offered it to my daughter, but she didn't want it and knocked it out of my hand; when I stooped to pick it up, she said she wanted black night. Two women carrying buckets joined us in the dark shadow of the trees; they glanced at me and began to laugh. One was young and tall with protruding eyes, like all the old women in the village. The other was short, her braided hair falling across her breast, all the way down to her waist. They approached the fountain, the protruding eyes staring straight at me, laughing all the while. The whole village had done the same, ever since the child was born. When the woman laughed, I sensed she was thinking the same thing the children did when they caught sight of me with the child and cried deformed, deformed with their hands cupped in front of their mouths, just as they had shouted, go with the ugly girl, the ugly girl. Now the children had grown up, and the youngest had learnt spiteful things from their elders. The braid was filtering the water when, all at once, she threw a handful on my child. She started to scream: a tiny, spark-size worm was curling and uncurling on her hand. The woman said my daughter was a child with corrupted blood. And a crybaby. They began talking to each other, but before they began to speak, I asked them how they would like to find a worm on their skin; they paid no mind. They talked as if they were on their own, but everything they said was for my benefit. They said both my wife and daughter bore withered arms. I had had the prettiest mother in the village, jealous of newlyweds, a woman who died, consumed by some kind of inexplicable rage. The braid stared at me with black eyes. She looked at me as though I were a tree or grass. She said I should be ashamed, should have been thrashed from time to time after my father had died, instead of disgracing myself by climbing into bed with my stepmother. The protruding eyes said my dead father had wanted an indecent death. They had killed his desire because they realized right away what he was doing . . . he was obstinate. And they couldn't finish killing him because his soul had enveloped him with such a dense mantle. The braid spoke up, so he went to bed with his stepmother who has a flowerpot with one bloom. The protruding, stark-white eyes doubled forward with laughter, and the braided one doubled backwards, laughing even harder, like two mad women. At that moment the ivy on the fountain shook. It was the blacksmith's son. The braid stopped laughing and shouted, you think we don't hear you, you think we don't see you, you think we don't know you spy on everyone. I'll tell your mother to strap you to the bed again. My child began to shout, come out, come out. As soon as the blacksmith's son jumped from the rock, he grabbed the braid's arm and stuck his face right up against hers and told her to leave me alone and hurry back to the village, the wisteria roots were upwrenching her house: two *Caramens* had come in the night to water them with the grass juice that makes them grow uncontrollably. The protruding eyes told him to stop plying them with stories and go back to the bed where he'd spent his whole life, where he should end it, and if his father was the leader of a group of people with stones for brains, her husband was a watchman, so the two men were about the same, maybe the watchman was a little better, he didn't pester anyone. The braid jerked her hand away from the boy, said he was always looking for excuses to touch her, told him to watch out because, scrawny as he was, one slap from her and he'd be knocked to the ground, and she'd make him fall with such fury that his flimsy, marrowless legs would break into three pieces: two to plug his eyes and the third to stuff his mouth. They picked up their buckets and strode off together, but they turned round after a moment, and the braid stuck out her tongue at us, crying, so you think you're as good as Senyor? Ha! My child was hugging the blacksmith's son's legs, telling him she wanted black night.

II

The blacksmith's son was five years younger than me. He had been frail since birth; the blacksmith's wife, she of the purple cheek, said it was better that way. He had lived all his life shut away, lying in bed. Only in the last year had he been allowed to go wherever he wished. It wasn't clear if he had lived in bed because he was ill or because his bones were soft. He would speak in a low, hoarse voice – like the prisoner's – that rose from deep inside him. Sometimes he would stop talking when he tired and breathe deeply, a sort of music emerging from inside him. He had coarse, blonde hair, a bit darker at the back of his head. When he talked for a long time, the first two fingers on one hand would spread apart the fingers on the other, as if he wanted to tear loose the skin where the fingers joined. He always said he had learnt many things from lying in bed so much. So much time to think. The day I first took my child to the forest of the dead, he jumped out in front of me without my hearing him; he had never spoken to me before. He told me he had been following me for days because I had entered his house one night when all the village had gone to a funeral; ever since then my hand seemed to accompany him. He told me I had touched him. He said before I left I leaned over to look at him, but he didn't know how to speak then; his tongue wasn't strong enough to form words because he had been forced to grow without food, so that he would always be ill and not have to swim under the village, not when he was young or old. He wanted me to touch his arm, said it was like a corpse even though blood flowed through it, like a dead person's arm because all the flesh had fled, everything that helped him to move it had vanished. Ever since the night he spoke to my child about souls – less than a year before – my child had loved him more than me. From the time she had the use of reason, she only wanted to be mine. The day he appeared before me in the forest, by surprise, without my hearing him, he told me he knew more things than I did because I had always been able to eat according to my appetite. He said he knew who turned the forest of the dead upside down, who played with the bones, and he never told anyone, but he asked me if one day I would open up a tree – he would help me – because he wanted to examine some leg bones, learn how knees bent in order to walk. My child was looking at a butterfly that had just been born; when the blacksmith's son realized, he caught it and put it in my girl's hand. She laughed and looked at him for a long time with quiet eyes. When we separated, she wanted to go with him instead of coming home with me. One night he explained to her all about souls, described what they did. After that they were inseparable. I heard him telling her. One evening when we had gone to see the prisoner, my child wandered off without our realizing; a while later the blacksmith's son got up to look for her, saying he would bring her back. They had been gone for a long time, so I went in search of them and found them at Pedres Altes. He was stretched out on top of the sundial, my child sitting on his chest, her feet on his neck, sometimes putting her foot in his mouth to make him be quiet. I listened from behind a large rock as the blacksmith's son explained to her that all souls went to the moon. Souls went to the moon. I watched them. My child's mouth was agape, and the blacksmith's son placed a finger inside her mouth and told her again that all souls went to the moon. All the ones that emerged from an uncemented mouth, because the ones that had lived inside people whose mouths were cemented couldn't escape. He said it wasn't exactly that souls could fly, but if they took a big leap, they were able to soar upward. He said they departed one at a time, sometimes joining up with others, like soap bubbles often do if you blow them one after the other. Occasionally, he said, they would catch the cloud cart pulled by the oldest souls, just like horses. They would go up and down, faster than mourners, and no one knows this – just like no one knows when the white birds fly away – but when they can no longer see the earth, it means they're approaching the moon. My child asked him what souls were like, and he told her there was no real way of knowing, and she wasn't supposed to tell anyone, he would tell only her – if it was even possible to explain. They were like a breath, a luminous breath in dark night. They fly up, he told her, and when they get close to the moon they go half mad with joy, like the birds when they fly down from the mountain, but just the opposite, because souls fly up. And they are so happy they don't know what they are doing, and they jump into the moon, and those that haven't got up enough speed – because they're tired, the voyage lasts a thousand years – fall back to earth. Some have time to grab onto an edge of the moon, and if they are strong enough, they remain there, and if not, they tumble down, and it's as if they had never even started their ascent. The ones that fly round and round on Maraldina are the ones that are waiting, or the ones that have fallen. He told her that on the moon there were patches of white grass, the most tender of all grasses – more tender than anything that could possibly be tender – because it was always half-grown. The best souls – that's when my child told him to be quiet – the best souls reach the center of the moon, not the edges, and they bore through it as if it were made of fog, and the souls that are waiting for them see them bounding up from the earth like a new sprout. Then he told her, yes he did, he told her that the oldest souls could eat the grass; they ate it through a horn in the middle of what had been their forehead . . . all of them aslant, eating grass . . . all of them, he told her, all of them aslant, eating grass in the pastures until they come to the river that goes round and round, no beginning, no ending, the river's mouth biting its tail. The ones that want to drink water drink water, and as soon as they've drunk they don't remember a thing. Not about you, not about me. Not about anything. The little they have inside them dies. If they suffered hunger, they don't remember what it means to be hungry; if they slept very little, they don't remember what it means to sleep. At first they're calm when they don't remember a thing, but soon they begin to feel uneasy; they don't know what it is, and no one explains to them why they feel like that . . . my child put her feet in his mouth and fell backwards, and he leaned up a bit and laughed as he took hold of her, telling her he wasn't finished. He told her that in the colored arc that forms in the sky after the rain, souls were lining up, waiting to take the cart. I can see them heading to the moon. The part where the colors spread and blend together, that part's full of souls. My child stuck a blade of grass in his mouth and said, eat – she had picked the blade near the prisoner's cage. And he ate it, confessing that after so many years without food, the more he ate the thinner he got. He continued talking – night was well under way and he spoke very slowly, as if he had to think before releasing any words. He explained to her that while soap bubbles were forming inside canes, they were being filled with souls; when one burst, it was because the soul had blown on it, and it escaped all sad-like. Sad. The bubbles that turned to glass held a soul inside: the bubble was the cage, you blow on it and it doesn't break. My child was laughing and putting blades of grass in his mouth, and he was chewing them, swallowing them down, pretending it was really hard to do so.

I emerged from my hiding place, and they glanced at me. He kept on explaining to her as if I wasn't there, all souls are good, evil things are done with hands and eyes, they don't have any of that, only one thing, they are souls and they can create wind. They blow, creating the wind, and the wind rushes through the heather and pushes men down the mountain, then up, because the souls that are waiting and the ones that have fallen to earth are sad, they want no part of anything, never again any part of this world. So they blow.

III

On our way to visit the prisoner, he told me that if we got in the habit of seeing each other, we'd learn a lot, he liked learning. The prisoner wouldn't tell him much because he knew he was the blacksmith's son, but if the two of us visited him together, he'd reveal a lot of things. My wife didn't want to come. She'd come a couple of times, but she soon grew tired of visiting him, because the prisoner frightened her; she said she dreamt about him at night and she had trouble getting up the following day. But she didn't want to come because she didn't like the blacksmith's son; he felt it, and, just to upset her, he'd call her deformed. As we were walking toward the wash area, the blacksmith's son told me it wasn't true that the worms from the fountain bored through skin; years ago someone had duped the village and everyone had believed it. If worms emerged from the prisoner's skin after he'd drunk water, it was because he really believed it was true. All the things you truly believe occur. You'll see, he said. I was weary of the blacksmith's son, but I liked the tract of land after the wash area, where the ground slopes down, narrows, then comes to a halt in a sharp point between the cleft mountain and the river. From there you could see Pedres Altes and Maraldina, and on the other side of the river closer to us, the trees lining the path that led to Font de la Jonquilla, ivy leaves above our heads, a trace of wind making them sing from top to bottom.

As soon as the prisoner saw us, he spread his arms and legs, tilting his head as if he were dead. The blacksmith's son poked his ribs, told him he had to be punished, told him his father had ordered it because he hadn't neighed in several days and the whole village really enjoyed his neighs. He made him drink water from a jar he'd brought from home; he'd filled it with water from the river once we'd passed the wash area. The prisoner swallowed it, and when he opened his mouth as if he were going to neigh, the blacksmith's son threw more water down his throat, as though his mouth were a bucket. The prisoner choked and coughed, his tongue hanging out of his mouth, the veins on his neck all swollen. To stop the choking the blacksmith's son had him drink more water; then he finished the little that was left. We sat down on the ground, but I had to jump up to seize my child; she was trying to thrust her head between the bars of the abandoned cage that was a little ways off: she had it halfway in and couldn't get it out. The prisoner sat very still, hardly breathing. After a while he began to groan, and the blacksmith's son said, you see? Look at me, I drank the same water and nothing's happened to me. His mouth smelled of slime. I could still catch the stench of slime when the prisoner threw himself on the ground. My child nudged one of his feet, and the blacksmith's son told her not to touch the prisoner because he was rabid. In the darkness the prisoner appeared to have two little specks on his arm surrounded by a bit of juice, like blood mixed with water. The blacksmith's son looked at me and kept saying, I don't have a thing. It only happens to him because he believes in it; the worms go down you and die, they don't hurt you, I drink water from Font de la Jonquilla all the time, as much as I want. He stood up, took the prisoner's head with both his hands, and told him the water he'd drunk didn't have worms, he shouldn't believe the stories. In exchange for what he was revealing, he should tell us what they do to kill desire; he'd asked many people, many times, and no one wanted to tell him. The prisoner looked down at his arm and shook his head; the blacksmith's son took hold of his head, pulled his hair, and we left.

Alone and bored while my child and the blacksmith's son roamed through the fields of black night or the forest or Pedres Altes, I would visit the prisoner. I'd sit by his side, and when I was tired of being there, I'd leave. One day, without my asking him anything, he spoke. He told me you had to live pretending to believe everything. Pretending to believe everything and doing everything others wanted; he'd been imprisoned when he was young because he knew the truth and spoke it. Not the truth of the faceless men. The real thing. The only person I felt close to was the prisoner. With my wife it was always the same – she couldn't abide me – and the child was crazy, infatuated with the blacksmith's son. I would wait until the wash women had left, and then I'd sit close to the prisoner. His fingers and toes were very long, his bones covered with dark skin, shriveled from being exposed so much to the sun, cold, and wind. Sometimes I'd find him half asleep, weary from neighing and listening to the women screaming at him, ordering him to neigh. His voice was different when he talked to me. It became human. He told me the burden of life came from the fact that we sprang partly from earth, partly from air. He was silent a moment, then told me not to keep company with the blacksmith's son because his mother was a beast. Then he repeated: part air, not like fish that are only from water. Or like birds that are from the air. One married to water, the other married to air. Man is made of water, lives with earth and air. He lives imprisoned. All men. He explained that when the villagers came to gaze at him, exhibiting him to their children, they all said he's a prisoner, but he wasn't a prisoner, he said, he lived differently from others, only that. He'd grown accustomed to living that way, and when they removed the cage because they thought he was no longer a person, it was all the same to him. So he stayed. Nothing mattered to him, living behind bars or with no bars. He was his own prison. Everyone bears their own prison, nothing changes, only habits, from listening so long to the coursing river, he said, and from seeing so much water drift past. What drifted past was him. I flow past, he said, everything else remains. Man lives between earth and air, is made of water, and lives imprisoned like the river that has earth beneath it and air above. The river is like a man. Always along the same appointed path, and if at times the river overflows, like a man's heart when he can no longer bear it, a law returns it to its course. He spoke without looking at me.

He could only look in front of him – with red-ringed eyes consumed by fire – as if he couldn't turn his head, as if what bound head to shoulder had grown rigid. To look at me – the few times he did so – he would turn his whole body, groaning as if his bones caused him pain. When things were calm and he felt part of the flowing river of life – like a wave of wind in the ivy leaves – he would raise a hand and listen with his eyes shut. When he spoke again, his words seemed to flow above the water, cleaved, partially destroyed. He felt them fleeing and said, everything I say, everything I say, everything I have said is carried away by the water, abandoned. Neither men nor women can feel what I'm describing. He said it was all a lie. Before, they didn't want to hear what he said, and now he doesn't want to speak. Everything they say is a lie: those that say that a serpent changed into water . . . they want to believe, need to believe, that if a mouth is cemented, the person's soul remains in the body. They need to believe that the pregnant women won't fall in love with other men, and their children will look like their fathers, if their eyes are bandaged. They don't know that if they bind their eyes it's because the child is already ill before being born. They don't see this, but what I speak is true. They believe they must swim under the village and must die in doing so. The village can only be settled above the river, instead of at Pedres Altes or by the forest; the cemetery only placed at the edge of Maraldina. And the shadows of the *Caramens* that no one has ever seen: no one has ever seen a shadow, no one knows if the *Caramens*' village is a village or a cloud. The watchmen are on guard, but what they guard against is nowhere to be seen. They continue to mutilate men because they say two shadows once joined together. It's fear. They want to be afraid. They want to believe, and they want to suffer, suffer, only suffer, and they choke the dying to make them suffer even more, so they'll suffer till their last breath, so that no good moment can ever exist. If the rocks and water rip away your face, it's for the sake of everyone. If you live with the belief that the river will carry away the village, you won't think about anything else. Let suffering be removed, but not desire, because desire keeps you alive. That's why they're afraid. They are consumed by the fear of desire. They want to suffer so they won't think about desire. You're maimed when you're little, and fear is hammered into the back of your head. Because desire keeps you alive, they kill it off while you're growing up, the desire for all things, in that way when you're grown . . .

While he was speaking, night fell, and I returned home, taking my time as I walked along the streets, everything asleep. I thought about the blacksmith's son. One day he told me he could feel when desire wafted through the village. Desire weighed on his chest, the same heaviness and troubled spirit in his blood as when a storm was brewing. I stopped in front of doors, and in the darkness I could make out the large black smudges left by so many hanging birds. One night, as I lay in bed listening to the flow of the river, I felt it was true; I was like a river with the earth below and air above. The true river had stopped, and I was the one who flowed farther and farther away, all alone in the center, trees on both sides. Then the prisoner spoke to me of desire.

Not the desire of children, who want everything, he said. All the women in the village have long hair. Here he stopped that first day. He stopped at the beginning. When he'd finished explaining, I couldn't see his face, only the shadow of his head, like the night above the cemetery of the uncemented dead, when I could see only the shadow of my stepmother's hair. All of them have long hair until . . . and when they desire a man, if her husband realizes it, if he realizes, he said, then he begins to stroke his wife. He does everything she wishes. Everything. And while he's doing everything she wishes, one day he takes her, sits her on his lap, and places his lips against her neck. But first he takes her hair and gently moves it away from her neck, brushing her hair aside; some strands slip away, fall, and he picks them up again until no hair remains on her neck. Then he places his lips on her neck and tells his wife to say the name. The name. He asks and asks. The wife won't tell, doesn't tell him. No. Some of them almost die. Finally, some wives, drowsy from the gentle kisses and the soothing feeling on their hairless skin, tell their husbands. The prisoner spoke softly, so softly I had to move closer in order to hear, and I realized I was doing the same thing as the blacksmith's son: with the first two fingers on one hand I was spreading the fingers on the other, almost tearing the skin at the joints. He told me they'd killed my father's desire after my mother turned ugly, when she screamed the loudest at the newlyweds, before he brought my stepmother home. He said they'd killed my father's desire, and that of many in the village. The village was full of them, and when they've killed your desire, they look at you tenderly, all happy, as if you were a child. A man and a woman, he said, walk past each other on the street and look at each other. It's the birth of desire. When desire is killed in old men they seem more dead than others. When the husband has forced out the name, he makes his wife lie on the bed and has the other man brought to him, makes him lie next to his wife, and stands at the foot of the bed watching. If the wife has given the other man's name, he can't refuse to obey the woman's husband. They can look at each other but they can't speak. It depends on the kind of woman: some won't look, others won't stop looking, and, as time elapses, her husband at the foot of the bed becomes more and more of a man. And the two who are lying down become less and less man and woman with each passing moment, till finally the day arrives when the woman covers her face with her hands and screams. This is how they kill desire, bit by bit, if need be. The longest phase lasts an afternoon. If the woman doesn't scream, there's another afternoon. Sometimes this lasts for months, if the husband encounters strong desire. When the woman screams, desire flees from the hearts of the man and woman. I had it. It was born, I don't know how. I did everything I could so they wouldn't notice. I didn't look. But they discover it in your eyes. Don't look. They guessed it in the woman, and I knew she wouldn't be able to bear it and would reveal my name right away. I could feel it stretched out in bed, ill all over. I don't know how, but I could feel the weight of her hair as it slipped between her husband's fingers, again and again. It was worse than listening to the river flow, day and night, worse than neighing. Worse than everything. It was as if every strand of hair that his hand brushed away was strangling me, each hair one day of my life, a fleeting day, while I lay still and salt water streamed from my body, out of my pores. Look at all the men in the village whose desire has been killed; they have eyes like horses that don't know when they're living and when they're slaughtered. They are the ones who stand in front of the others when they come to gaze at me. They're like me.

IV

For some time I couldn't rid myself of the blacksmith's son, so I began doing everything I could to avoid encountering him. I left the house when I knew he was coming. I stopped going to the places I used to frequent. I would pretend to go down one path, then cut off to another. He appeared everywhere, as if I had told him where I was going before even I had decided. My child would wander aimlessly if she wasn't with him; and if she spent a whole day without seeing him, she would throw herself on me, scratch me, crying that she wanted him, wanted black night. When we slept, she would sneak out, and I would have to search the village streets to find her. I finally had to let it be, and when I allowed them to do whatever they wanted, then the blacksmith's son spoke of the green window. I could tell he was happy to talk about it because he sensed I was weary of him, and while he talked he stared at me with a leaden look, pretending he was sorry to tell me these things, but happy inside that he could. I began to know him. He carried about him all the rancor of having suffered the life he had been forced to live. Without my wishing it, he knew how to draw me to his side. For some time he told me that I was a hand to him, repeating it so often that I couldn't stop thinking about it. It entered my blood. When he sensed I was snared, he breathed deeply, and I shriveled up. I would take hold of my daughter and ask her whose child she was, and when my child said she was his, she looked at me for a long, long time without blinking, her eyes like still water. He asked me if I had ever looked behind the green window. I have, he said. I had never wished to grab him and kill him as much as that day. Often I had had to restrain my desire to kill him, push him off the Pont de Fusta into the river, strike him with an axe as if he were a tree of the dead. He told me in the red-powder cave, where for a long time he had wanted to go, but not alone. He told me, sitting on the ground, my child on his lap, breathing in the crimson powder – a lot had recently fallen from the ceiling, and a mound of it lay near the opening my stepmother and I had made to gain entrance to the second well. Everything smelled of powder and heather-earth. My child had fallen asleep, and he was stroking her hair, gently, almost without touching her. I told him another well existed, where you could hear the river flowing, but the water from that river had no outlet. If it had, the water would have been red when it surfaced the day we threw so much powder in it. He said the mud-flower pond lay beyond the tree cemetery, hidden in the growth at the end of the marsh, and the water in the pond was always half-red. The flowers bore the color of the water, as if in order to grow they had drunk from it. The pond was bloody from the red powder and the horses and old men from the slaughterhouse. He said he'd looked carefully at my house. As soon as he was able to leave his bed, he said, I started looking at things slowly because my eyes couldn't hold so many new things at the same time. I wanted to see things; I knew nothing. Not about grasses or other people's faces. You can't imagine what it is to never see another person other than your parents, then to see a face and glimpse it in the open air, by yourself. When I was little, people would come to stare at me, but then they stopped coming, and the only thing I saw was the wall of ivy, a swarm of those creatures that make honey, my father's crooked legs, my mother's purple cheek. I wasn't hungry, I wasn't hungry, nor will I ever be again, but my eyes' hunger will always exist . . . those twigs the day we lay on the ground, the ones we saw in front of the fog, we saw only the twigs, as if everything were dead. He had said, look at them, they're swimming in the air in front of the fog, but there is no air, and if you stare at them long enough you can't tell what they are, just thin streaks on fleeing water that's turned into fog. The wish to see comes from not knowing anything. I could only remember you. And you, you're a hand. The first night I was able to stand and walk a bit – because they fed me – I went in search of your house, the hottest night of all, a snake hidden in the courtyard under a sack. They said the wisteria was tilting the houses, and I grew uneasy, afraid your house would collapse. No birds were strung on the doors; I'd imagined all the doors with birds hanging by their feet. The leaves were yellow, the wall just beginning to turn red. This was the only thing I knew about plants: some leaves turned yellow, others red. Later, I lifted the curtain. I could see nothing. Later still, I learnt that your house had a worn step, the one in the middle. The transparent leaves on both the white and red flowers had thick veins. I know, he said – I can still hear him – when they opened up your father's tree, his fingertips were red, his hair standing straight up. I know the wisteria trunk bears three incisions that your mother carved with a knife. I know what my father said when your father died. One word from a mouth is enough for me to guess everything. They say the prisoner tells lies. Do you believe it? And that my father is right. Do you believe it? I've learnt a lot, yet I can tell you I know nothing, only this: what happens is what counts. I felt he was uttering many of the things I thought, almost as if he were me. Maybe he had become me, from so many years of thinking about me as he lay in bed, lived in bed. He said, they all come, all of them. Everyone knows, you too. Your door is an open door. They go in and out. I tell you everyone knows. You've always known, from the time your father was still living. No one would want them because they stink of blood. Everyone keeps quiet about it because it suits them. You're afraid to look. You were afraid to look, and you know nothing. You don't know what she does: she fastens a rope round their necks. Playing. She's always liked to play. They become little again when they're with her. She ties a rope round their necks, he said, and she lies on the bed and makes them go round and round, one side to the other; the faster they run, the happier she is, but she doesn't laugh – I've never seen her laugh – until finally the old men tire. The one I saw was tall and fat, with a sunken chest and soft hands. He was like a horse. Have you noticed that the men in the village look like horses? I realized as soon as I saw a group of them together . . . and she'd pull on the rope or loosen it, sometimes moving her lips, never allowing a word to escape, but you could see she was saying, gitty . . .

We left the well. Outside, a gust of wind filled our eyes with earth, and we started walking, the wind bending us. When we reached the bottom, he said, you knew. Then we headed to Pedres Altes and sat on the sundial, contemplating the night. The following day he taught me how to make fire with two dry branches.

V

In a cave behind Pedres Altes lived the man with the cudgel. His palms were scarlet from swinging his cudgel on so many nights. The cudgel was his defense; he earned his living from it. He was old and no longer agreed to daily fights with boys from the village. The townspeople sent him boys one by one, and he received them, cudgel in hand. He was a tall man, taller than all of them. His hair was thinning, part-white, part-yellow. His toenails were like horse hooves: long and hard. Black. Because he walked through the manure pit near his cave to breathe in the stench, drawing strength from it. He had been trained in this manner since he was a child. To live patiently. A boy from the village awoke feeling brave one morning, wanting to devour sky and river, and asked to be allowed to fight the man with the cudgel. With his long, razor-sharp cane, the boy went in search of the old man, calling him out of his cave, challenging him, jumping and running about. The man emerged slowly, asked the lad what he wanted, knowing full well he wanted to battle; when the boy declared that he had come for combat, to defeat him, the man picked up the cudgel with both hands, lowered his head, and announced that they could begin. He opened his legs wide, planting himself firmly on both feet, and began to dodge the cane. Sometimes the cane grazed his skin, but he felt nothing. The combat continued until the boy fell to the ground, out of breath, half-dead, at which point, without even a glance at the lad, the man entered the cave to wait for night, when he would practice with his cudgel on the spot where the boy had fallen. The boy returned to the village a different person. If his blood had boiled before, now it had grown calm. He lived life better now than he had before. They said the man in the cave turned weak men strong.

When he fought, he made a sort of shrill sound with his tongue, and his lips grew soft. When he came out at night to swing his cudgel in the air, he clamored for the poisonous river serpent to rise up, the mountains to flatten, man to die before birth. He would swing his cudgel from left to right, right to left, upward, then down, his body hardly moving. He controlled everything with his arms, they said, and with a look that rose from deep inside. He had lived in the cave for more than fifty years. Almost all the men in the village had endured the trial of the cudgel. They took him food and manure – silently, so as not to wake him if he were asleep.

The blacksmith's son said he wanted to visit the man with the cudgel. We left the child asleep on top of the stone clock and circled Pedres Altes. At the entrance to the cave stood a clearing surrounded by high grass and shrubs. We caught sight of him right away, straight as a tree, swinging the cudgel above his head. He was uttering things we couldn't understand because he spoke in a low voice, but we caught the word *round* and the word *wind*. They said patience had made him strong, the patience to live a life swinging his shiny cudgel – shiny from being held so often – and defeating the village boys. While we watched him, he swung the cudgel from side to side at shoulder level; then slowly he stooped to knee level. If any legs had been within reach, he would have smashed them. We saw him stop and enter the cave, by this time his body bent from weariness, as if putting aside the cudgel had made him instantly grow old, his backbone soft. Not many boys from the village wanted to fight him. The elderly said that all the good things were fast vanishing.

I found myself alone. The blacksmith's son had disappeared; I didn't hear him leave. The night had been clear, but clouds began to form, and a diaphanous fog rose above the river and remained there. While I was gazing at it, suddenly – without my realizing it – the blacksmith's son appeared at my side again, telling me we had to hurry. I've taken the old man's cudgel and hidden it in the shrubs; let's leave before he notices. I think it was that very morning that I went down to the river to look for cane. The blacksmith's son had collected my daughter and taken her home. The fog didn't dare thicken; its drowsiness put the water to sleep. I headed to the Festa esplanade. It wasn't yet dawn, but a brighter ribbon of light gleamed from the sun side, and I was thinking about the man with the cudgel and how it had turned his palms scarlet, as if they were covered in blood.

VI

By the esplanade the river vaulted underground, creating a wave; but the water by the canes was calm. I sat down on a bench, my arms on the table, my head on my arms. I shut my eyes as if I were dead. I was dead. I would have stayed there all my life, until the wind scattered my dust. I could envisage my body, no longer flesh, turning first into sulphur dust that caught on the underside of bees, then into earth, and finally breathing new life into flowers. Once my existence unraveled, it became death and flew about; from spring to spring only winter's death would live. All of me was weighted down. As I was feeling the weight, I heard a splash and raised my head. Rings had formed in the water, giving birth to other rings, as if someone had hurled a flat rock. The rings kept spreading until they reached the point where they died. The days-old water was green on the opposite bank, where I had watched the Festa years before. When all the rings stopped, I glimpsed a hand by the canes. A hand above the water, as if supported from below, tiny and white and flat like a fearless spider. The hand rose, then fell furiously, striking the water. I approached the canes and hid. I caught sight of a girl who climbed out of the water and got dressed; she reappeared from behind the canes, tucking her bodice into her skirt, her back to me, the hem of her skirt almost grazing my knee. Her feet were pale. And the lower part of her legs. Her heels were rose-colored, like the pink houses in spring. When the bodice was tucked in, she took a few steps, stopped, looked at the sky, then dashed back to the water she had just abandoned and began waving her hand from one side to the other as she blew away the illusion of fog that wasn't really there. Just a bit of smoke. She returned to where she had been standing, but faced me this time and, raising her arms, she grasped her hair with both hands, pulled it up and tied it. As she lifted her arms, her bodice again escaped her skirt, and again she tucked it in. At that moment, without giving it a thought, without wanting to, I got to my feet. We looked at each other. She stood in front of me, her hands still raised, I in front of her. Both of us standing. Eye to eye, mouth to mouth, our hearts troubled. Not wanting to, not thinking, I stretched out my open hand, wishing to touch her because she was alive, yet wondering if she was real. As if I had passed on to her the wish to do what I had done, she extended her arm toward me, her hand open. That was enough. The two of us standing, our finger-tips on the verge of touching, barely separated by what might have been the thickness of a leaf. We remained like that as the morning mist grew thinner, as if the water in the middle of the river had swallowed it, instead of spitting it out. And she departed. I stood there with my hand outstretched. I jumped with a start when her hair abruptly came loose and fell like sudden night down her back. You, you are a hand, the blacksmith's son had told me. I stepped forward, placing my feet on the water spots she had left on the ground and pressed the soles of my feet as hard as I could against the earth, my body weightless. Her short, wet hair, was swept up, away from her neck. This is what I most remembered about her, before her hair fell loose. All the women in the village have long, fine hair. Her husband takes hold of her hair, a strand of which dangles free. I felt the birth of desire as I had never felt it, desire alone, violent and solitary as a rock. Look at them, their eyes like horses', never knowing when they live, when they die.

I gathered some canes and was heading back when I encountered a group of men leaving the village. I didn't look at them. As I was approaching the first street, I had a glimpse of the blacksmith's son running toward me. His father wanted to see me right away. I handed him the canes, told him to take them home, and hurried to the blacksmith's.

VII

The blacksmith needed me to deliver a message: he was unable to visit Senyor. He explained how to make the journey up to Senyor's house: after the bridge, the middle path. Three paths converged just beyond the bridge. One followed a difficult stretch through rock and water, ending in the village opposite some courtyards and rock. Another led to the flatlands. The path in the middle gave the appearance of being level but soon began to climb. I set out alone. My child was no doubt at Pedres Altes with the blacksmith's son. Dusk was falling. As I made my way up the mountain, it quickly grew dark below, but the higher land was still enveloped in light. The wind swirled whirlpools of dust. The village fields and stables lay to my right, Senyor's land – flat and endless – to my left. I told the blacksmith that Senyor might not believe his lie – that he couldn't scale the mountain because he'd fallen in the courtyard – but the blacksmith replied that Senyor believed everything. The prisoner had told me that all the women in the village had long, fine hair, all of them. Soon the stables and esplanade were hidden and only the river was visible, still calm without the fury of melting snow. A pregnant woman was bounding down the path. She was almost beside me before I noticed her. The sound of her footsteps lasted a while, then faded. When I could no longer hear them, I turned back to look at her, but she was merely an earth-colored shadow blending into the earth. I realized then that her eyes weren't bandaged, and I stopped to think about it. Higher up the air carried different, fresh smells. Two round rocks were planted in the ground on each side of the entrance. One was poorly set and leaned to the side. Above the door hung the stone coat of arms: at the top two birds faced each other; the rest was a bed of wisteria. I entered the patio. Several torches were blazing at eye level; a mourner was perched beneath each, half the number as on the coat of arms. I felt as if I had seen it all before. As I pondered the fact that I had witnessed this somewhere, I realized the impression sprang from the torches: the same torch flames that had made the low-hanging leaves glow that night in the tree cemetery. The sky was like that night, only now the butterflies had not yet been born. From the patio I glanced up. I could see a sliver of a moon; it was the same color as the sharp edge of the axe, and both ends curled toward the center. A man approached and asked what I wanted. I spoke to him of the blacksmith, and he immediately called to a woman who emerged from a little door and disappeared through the large one. She was gone a long time; when she returned she said Senyor was waiting for me. The woman led me down a wide corridor, through a very large room and another corridor, until we finally arrived at a long, narrow room that smelled of smoke from the extinguished fire. At the far end, in a black armchair, sat Senyor. As soon as he saw me he squinted to bring me into focus, said he knew me, had known my mother, I was beginning to look like her. He burst into a coughing fit and the glass in the window shook. When he stopped coughing, his chest rising and falling heavily, he asked about the blacksmith, and I explained about the fall. He had tears in his eyes from coughing and wiped them with a finger, shaking them away from the armchair. His upper lip curled a moment; then with both hands – which immediately turned whiter with the effort – he took hold of the arms of the chair to lift himself. When he was halfway up he sat back down, saying he couldn't remember why he wanted to get up. His upper lip rose after every word and trembled slightly round the corners of his mouth. He said perhaps he could tell me what he needed to tell the blacksmith, since the blacksmith had sent me instead. He had known my mother. His remarks were all jumbled. He told me he had been forced to live like that, had been given that kind of life, but when he was little they didn't prick his ear because his mother said he had enough with his twisted feet. He said maybe it would have been better if they'd left him completely empty. When he was little he always looked at people's feet, didn't know which feet were the proper ones, until little by little, thinking about it as he grew up, he came to realize that everyone had feet the way they should. Everyone except him. Then he was quiet for a long time, touching his knees. The moon – the skeleton of the moon – settled in front of the window; and finally Senyor said, when you've had to live, he said, when you've had to live with your lower body deformed, a man could at least choose his own way of dying. The prisoner – he called him the man in the cage – the man in the cage knew me, he was the bravest, forever looking straight in front of him, he'd always say: since you can't choose the way you live, you should at least be able to choose the way you die, and you should finish . . . But I can't finish anything; there are things you can't do unless someone helps you, and these things include dying the way you wish, when you wish. Death is always ugly, those worms that have hatched within you, waiting for you, the worms of patience that do their work fast – when they can – and do it well. The man in the cage had to endure hours and hours of torment, of having his desire killed off. One day they told me he'd wanted to end his life, he wanted to end his life, he lived without living, always thinking about himself and about the village, as if the village was him and he the village. As soon as they locked him up, I think he began to live because he could no longer wish for anything, everything came from others rather than from himself . . . like what they did with your father. I didn't find out for a long time. On this side of the mountain things are always chipped and dented when they reach us because of a sort of rupture built up over the years, but even so, news of everything reaches us in the end. Some people want to change things, maybe they're right, it's all the same to me. Now that I'm old, I only wish for one thing, to die with an empty mouth. I don't want to die like your father, because what they did to him . . . I don't want to die the way they force you to die. The closer I get, the less I want it and the more I think about it. He made me describe my father's last death. From time to time, he placed a hand before his mouth, and his fearful eyes peered at me above the hand. I explained how they had pulled him from the tree, black night filled with shouts, everyone carrying a torch, a drop of saliva running with delight from the corner of an old man's lip, how they had finished him off. He told me I was young; when he was young the villagers never glimpsed his eyes because he so rarely went down the mountain. Then he said: that's what kept me alive, never stopping, never stopping, one woman after another, always preferring the other one. I didn't know then what was inside a man, and when I discovered, I wanted to die. With un-focused eyes he said: accompanied by the wish to live, you have the wish to die; it'll be like that till the end. Spring is sad, in spring all the world is ill, plants and flowers are earth's plague, rotten. The earth would be calmer if it were green-less, without this fury, this blind will that consumes everything but craves more, the afflic-tion of the green, so much greenness and poisonous color. When the wind drives everything from one end of the world to the other, seeds and particles and everything it covets, then men become tormented. Birds contribute to this, so do bees – they carry so much sulphur dust, caught on their backs, their legs, nothing carries as much sulphur dust as bees. The man in the cage used to say, kill the wisteria, he said it often, I know they spread honey on him, he'd often say that, he was truly a man, now they say he's thin as a cane, his brain twisted round. One morning you'll get up thinking that the things you carry within you have died, but it won't be true; when you think this has happened it'll really be you who has died a bit. Things don't die. They continue. They pass from one to another, always in this fashion, from one to another. He waved his open hand from right to left, a worn hand, covered with blemishes, fingers stiff at the joints, the hands of a very old man. Always from one to the other, like water from the sky that falls to earth, like fog that rises from the water, like seeds and particles. The mourners come, then the white birds arrive and end up hanging from doors. The mourners leave, and the horses call out to them. I have come only to leave, for that reason alone.

But I came without being able to walk like others, punished perhaps by those who first began to kill the horses, but I don't want
cement. I'm descended from the man who established the village.
Give me your hand. His hand was hot and dry. He broke out in a
coughing fit that was worse than the first. As soon as he could
speak, he pointed to a jar on a little table, saying he wanted some
honey. Dog roses were painted all across the white jar, and the
handle of a spoon, in the form of a serpent's tail, protruded from
it. He took a spoonful of honey, ate it little by little, said the honey
was bitter. Who knows what diseased flowers the bees have sucked?
Like women. The river said it had been a serpent – as he spoke he
plunged the spoon into the honey – the serpent . . . He broke off
to run his tongue over his lips, removing the honey stuck to them.
The first man who settled the village killed the serpent at the top
of the mountain, and flung it, flung it against the mountain, and
the mountain split. He was already dead. All of him was dead,
blood still flowing through him, but with the pallor of death on
his emaciated face, thin lips, and miraculously straight back. Men
who are eager to kill are men who are already dead. Men who do
things are men who are already dead. He was a man who was
already dead, could do only remarkable things, he and his horse
were one and the same because he'd passed on to his horse all of his
death, never realizing they were both dead from the first day they
began pursuing the serpent. The moment the serpent died, it
changed into water and coursed beneath the rocks that had come
hurling down. The man who had been dead inside, since the day
he first began to pursue the serpent, died on the outside, trampled
by his horse a few years later, down the mountain, at the bend in
the river, near the tree cemetery. He clutched my hand. When the
moon is round, you'll see the serpent scales above the water. In the
village you can still hear the neighing of the horse that went
mad – a man had passed his own death on to the horse by forcing
him to pursue the serpent time and time again. He squeezed my
hand, tighter and tighter. As his hot, mottled hand clasped mine, I
caught the scent of water and canes, the air barely clipped by a

hand approaching me. He said, with my hand in his, he could feel the weight of death, everything coming to an end. He held youth in his hand but couldn't retain it. Everything is ending: the light, my existence that still binds me to the earth, as the earth binds and envelops roots. He said things formed piles within him. The years too. Things become superimposed and each thing wants to be the first on your mind. Things pile up, the years too. The years are jumbled in our thoughts. At the moment of thinking, instead of thinking about the last years – the youngest – or thinking about the first ones – the oldest – he thought about the middle years, and within the middle years he jumped from one idea to another without restraint. Sometimes everything got jumbled, and he had to shut his eyes, one hand on each side of his forehead, his head was splitting open. Everything was choking him, sinking deep inside him, like the river engulfing the dead. But sometimes at night the water draws things upstream – sad, broken things, sadder than the white bird that appeared like a sigh, escaping out of the serpent's mouth at the moment of its death. A man never thinks what he'd like to think. Tell him that, you hear me? And he squeezed my hand. Tell him to come and help me, convince them, because I think like him. We're alike. Tell him to let me die, don't let me be killed. Tell him without telling him I told you. I've suffered enough. I couldn't walk like others, and one day I wanted to cut off my feet. But my heart stopped. The heart's like that. Moving his shirt aside, he had me place my hand on his chest. It never stops, always working. It's what keeps us alive. Sometimes it's tired and moves slowly, like a person; sometimes it stops with a furious tremor, sometimes it melts. My heart stopped when blood streamed across my feet. Then it began to gallop like a horse gone mad, leaving the impression that my heart had slipped deeper inside me, so as to beat more strongly later on. You tell him this and tell him not to fall again. Some falls are bad. One day you'll realize the heart must live alone; everything that envelops it is worthless. Mine has lived. If only you knew how it has lived from spring to blazing leaves and from blazing leaves to spring. He released my hand, having passed on to me his burning heat. Honey burns, he said, nothing burns as much as honey, even if it's made from diseased flowers. Tell him I'll see that he's notified, now leave. When you're a man, you'll choke like me and you'll remember my hand that was beginning to die, was thin, was no longer a hand.

But he had to die like everyone else. They made him die in the center of the Plaça. They wanted to watch him. When Senyor's eyes began to protrude, an old man from the slaughterhouse said: he wanted to see the village carried away by the river, and the village sees him carried away by death. And I didn't know where that girl was.

VIII

Everything was solitary and quiet as I walked back down the path. Groups of men were strolling through the streets. I could not rid myself of the fever that had passed to my hand, nor free my eyes of the image of Senyor's vacant eyes peering at me above his mottled hand as I described my father's last death. All of this merged with the images of the man who enjoyed watching people die and the woman shouting as she was led away. I approached one of the groups, where a man was explaining that early that morning – when the sun was scaling the stone arch, heading for the bend in the river – he had ventured close to the old man's cave and found the man with the cudgel standing in the center of the clearing, hands in the air, crying out to the stones and to all that could hear him – everywhere his voice could reach – that he was a dead man. I left the group and drew near another, where a man said that someone had stolen the cudgel from the old man of the cave. The man announced that if he discovered who had committed the deed, he'd drag his face through the dust, slash open his back with the old man's cudgel, and sow the ground with his blood. Another man said in a troubled voice that when he was young he'd fought against the patient old man, and after the contest the way he perceived life had changed. In front of the blacksmith's house, a large number of men were discussing whether it was a good thing to have troubled the old man, who'd had a difficult life. To steal his cudgel was to steal his hands. One mentioned that he could remember how the old man had won the cave when he was young by fighting against two cudgel-swinging men. He'd defeated the two of them without moving, stopping the blows of one and the other as they swung and tried to outwit him. Finally he'd delivered the death blow to both, and took possession of the cave, leaving the men at his feet, slain by killings as clean as handfuls of water. As the man uttered these last words beneath the heavy wisteria-laden night, I saw the hand without ever seeing it. The blacksmith's voice could be heard above the others', telling them there was no need to be so anxious: his son had just reported that the old man had recovered his cudgel. Go home to your houses, don't think of this any more. A youngish man, with black eyes and sunken cheeks, approached the blacksmith, placing his hand on the smithy's shoulder. The blacksmith turned his head, glancing at the hand on his shoulder, and looked into the man's eyes. If anyone torments the old man of the cave, announced the young man, they'll have to reckon with me. The day we battled, I sliced open the man of the cave's chest, and with blood gushing out of him, the only thing the old man did was stop my blows. When I fell to the ground, as everyone did – the man of the black eyes exclaimed – instead of wounding me, he left me with light, and patience pervaded all my being. He removed his hand from the blacksmith's shoulder and continued speaking: if anything bad should happen to the old man of the cave, I give my word that I'll kill the prisoner. He began to shout: that bag of bones and rancor, evil soul, worse than any of us. Another man, similar to him – black eyes and flattened hair – approached him, shaking his head from side to side, as if his words were directed at everyone, and he announced that he'd talked to the prisoner once about the man of the cave. The prisoner said if the men who ventured out to fight were unmanly after their mothers had mangled their ears, they were even less so after combat. It's hard to believe, the prisoner had told him, that no one recognizes the man of the cave's pride. He leaves the combatants half-dead and returns to his cave to laugh. The blacksmith told him to be quiet; he wanted to know if the prisoner had said this while he was still locked in the cage or when he'd ceased to be a person. The man couldn't respond because the man with the sunken cheeks struck him on the face with his fist, knocking him flat on the street. People cried out for the prisoner to be put back into the cage. The blacksmith raised his hand to calm the crowd, again telling everyone to go home. In the end nothing bad had occurred, the old man again had his cudgel, according to what his son had told him, and while everyone was worrying about the old man, he was sleeping like a rock. At that very moment a barely audible neighing sprang from the prisoner, and from out of the darkness a desperate neighing issued from one of the village streets. No one knew who had neighed.

When everyone had left, the blacksmith had me enter his house and by the forge asked me what Senyor had said. When I told him, he replied that he had imagined as much. While I was explaining everything Senyor had told me, he slowly ran a finger through the ashes, forming a furrow. Without cement! Don't they understand, like your father, that it's for their own good? To have a calm life beyond life, they must be complete, as they were before. Can't they see that? He moved away from the forge and picked up an iron bar that I would never have been able to lift, and, full of rage, began striking the anvil madly, shouting louder and louder: don't they understand? Don't they understand?

IX

A sense of unease swept through the village. I could feel it. The unease the blacksmith's son felt when too much desire troubled the inhabitants, weighing on his chest like a storm brewing behind the mountains. At night, the prisoner would tell me his life was drawing to an end; it was almost over. He had had his fill. The water, the ivy, the wash women who think of one thing only, laughing at me because they believe that I too think only about this thing. All the women waiting for night to fall, and this thing far away, carried off not by water but by my blood that has changed and changed, growing old and thick. He asked me if the blacksmith's son had hidden the old man's cudgel. I told him that when the cudgel was hidden, groups of men had gathered in the village to talk about it. The prisoner said they only wanted to wag their tongues. Years ago the villagers should have mistreated the man with the cudgel; he was useless. The only thing he did was shatter young people's strength and eagerness; the youth should thank him for wearing them out.

Two or three weeks after my visit to Senyor, a man came down the mountain and told the blacksmith to go up right away because Senyor wanted him close by, to help him die as he wished. The blacksmith made the climb with four or five other men, plus two very robust ones who carried a stretcher. I didn't realize until later, but I think it was at that point that evil was set loose and began to ravage the village. No one was able to stop its course. As the blacksmith moved through the village, he wore the same face as the day I told him my father had entered the tree and had most likely stopped breathing. He had seemed possessed as he rushed out to gather people. They strapped Senyor to the stretcher by his feet and wrists. It seems an argument developed on the mountain – some men didn't want Senyor to be brought down to the village. They said he should die in his own house. But the blacksmith and the men with him convinced them, with words or with blows. As the stretcher reached one end of the Plaça, the cement man arrived from the other side. Senyor looked at them all with yellow, dull eyes, as if the film covering them had been ripped away. Everyone was in the Plaça, the village crones in a corner by the shed where the paintbrushes were stored. The prisoner and horses began to neigh; no one had ever heard such a chorus of neighing, all at the same time, that lasted so long. The blacksmith gave the word for the cement man to commence; they forced open Senyor's mouth and began to fill it. Senyor's eyes were bulging; his chest rose twice as he retched. The man next to me described how they had gone up the mountain to fetch him. As soon as Senyor realized what they wanted, he jumped from his deathbed with frightening youthful force and tried to escape, but the blacksmith gave him a hard blow with his fist on the back of his neck and he lost consciousness. He came to his senses as they were carrying him down the mountain; they say he began to whimper, as if instead of mother and father he had had only a mother, for he whimpered more than any woman. Several young men approached the stretcher and attempted to untie Senyor; one of them grasped the cement man by the neck and would have strangled him if another man had not quickly knocked him to the ground, kicking him in the stomach. The villagers grabbed hold of the men who wanted to untie Senyor and placed them under guard near the old women. Senyor began to cough furiously, bringing up cement; a drop of blood fell on the ground, he had dug his fingernails into his palms. His body retched again; when it calmed he was dead. The pregnant women began to scream because several pregnant women from the mountain, whose eyes were unbound, wanted to remove their bandages. Throughout it all, the old women standing near the men who wanted to untie Senyor had spat and insulted Senyor as he lay dying. All except one, who went over to him, knelt down, removed the cement from round his mouth, and closed his now undiscerning eyes with her palms, so people would not see them. So people would not see the suffering eyes, the old woman had knelt in front of him and with her rough palms had pressed his eyes half closed, while there was still time she said. Everyone prepared to go to the forest. The men had already lifted the stretcher, their arms extended, the veins in the bend of their elbows taut.

The blacksmith announced that they would cage the prisoner when they returned from the burial.

X

The villagers left the Plaça: the men with the stretcher in front, the blacksmith leading everyone. They carried torches, but the last dregs of light could still be glimpsed behind Maraldina and the Muntanyes Morades. As soon as they had quit the village, the sound of galloping horses reached them from the right-hand side of Pedres Baixes. Everything came to a standstill, even before the blacksmith raised his hand, signaling them to stop. When the horses had almost reached the slaughterhouse, the blacksmith turned and exclaimed: the watchmen! Three men galloped up; their horses came to a halt before the stretcher and reared. Without dismounting, the middle watchman said this time it was certain. They had seen the *Caramens* at dawn, up close – impossible to be any closer – hiding in the shrubs, crouching and creeping from one shrub to another. You could hardly hear them, as if they didn't have legs. A loud rumble of voices rose at the back of the group because they hadn't heard a word. The man who had spoken pointed to the watchman on his right, saying, he saw them. The blacksmith asked if there were many of them; the middle watchman said it was hard to know but he thought so. The blacksmith turned and faced the villagers, telling them to go to their houses and look for arms with which to defend themselves. He sent the watchmen back and chose some men to follow them, to gather wood and build large bonfires between Pedres Baixes and Pedres Altes. Once night had fallen, if they received word that the shadows were approaching, they were to light the fires to frighten them away. He gave them some iron awls, longer than the ones they used to torment children's desire. The watchman who had seen the shadows said the horses were tired; they'd die if they had to make the return trip so fast. The blacksmith ordered them to be given fresh horses, and while everyone was returning to the village, he took me and a few others, saying the first thing we had to do was cage the prisoner. The blacksmith's wife and a few other women came with us, and when we approached the wash area, they began to laugh and poke each other with their elbows for no reason at all. The blacksmith gave his wife an angry slap across her purple mark and told her it wasn't the time to laugh, that would come later. He told her to go and rest, because the real party would begin when the *Caramens* attacked the village. The women were still, but didn't leave. The blacksmith talked to the prisoner, I can't remember what he said, something about not behaving as he should, all the village wanted to see him caged, and if after he was caged he spoke to the village boys of things he shouldn't, he'd find a way to punish his deceitful tongue. While the men looked from the prisoner to the blacksmith, I was watching the village and suddenly noticed smoke rising. At first, I didn't think anything about it; I looked at the smoke curling as it climbed and tried to imagine the men who had glimpsed the shadows in the shrubs. The smoke was like a black tree trunk rising in the air. I was surprised when I heard my voice saying that a house in the village was on fire, only I didn't say a house, I said the village, because it seemed to me that the whole village was burning; the shadows had set fire to the village while people was preparing to defend it. Everyone turned to look at the smoke, and the blacksmith's wife and the other women became agitated. It's hard for me to know, hard to think, hard to remember, hard to know in what order things happened, but in the end it all goes round, when I've forgotten it all, forgotten about me and everything else, and the fire returns. The blacksmith's house was on fire, and it was as if fire and wind inhabited it, and wind and fire poured out of the windows, at times in steady streams, other times in broken spells. A furious tongue of fire rose, then suddenly broke into deliquescent red and blue tongues, sometimes clear fire, sometimes crowned by smoke searching for its way through the air, not knowing which direction to take, until finally the wind carried it off. The fire cried out with a desperate voice, like a voice laughing at everything, crimson with madness. And the prisoner . . . no, it was then that they beat me, not one man alone, more than one, because it was my fault that the prisoner had killed himself. Some days later the blacksmith's son told me who had started the fire. The pain I felt when they were beating me merged with the smoke that was drawing flames with it as it fled; it all blended into the murmur of the water coursing beneath the village and the hands beating me. As we watched the smoke, the prisoner had let himself slip into the water; he went under and the river swept him away, at the spot where people went to gaze at the rocks. The blacksmith's son wasn't with us. He hadn't come to cage the prisoner. Nor was he in the Plaça while they were cementing Senyor. I woke up – or was regaining consciousness after the beating – and saw more houses burning. The fire leapt higher and higher, turning the sky scarlet, like tinted fog. My back ached, especially my right shoulder. I wiped my mouth and discovered clotted blood on one side. The taste in my mouth was one I'd never experienced before: dust and ashes and filthy water. I stood up and found myself alone. By the light of the fire, I could make out the place where the prisoner had let himself slide into the water when I shouted that the houses were on fire. I was just beyond the wash area, on my way back into the village, when I came across a frightened woman who, as she passed me, said they were killing her husband and she couldn't bear it any longer. Men were fighting in front of the blacksmith's house; my wife was seated in a corner, terrified, her hands covering her face. I walked toward them, and just as I reached the group, someone grabbed me by the neck, a man I didn't know. He told me some boys from the village had killed the man of the cave and I was part of it, because my wife had borne the news. He shook her by the shoulders. She said it was true, she'd heard shouts and had stopped, heard how the boys killed him, the old man groaning, the boys laughing. They killed him with his own cudgel. She ran to the village to give the news and discovered the burning houses. When the man asked her what she was doing near the cave, she said she'd gone to Maraldina to visit the cemetery where her mother was buried. She went there often, and when she came back she always took the long route, to see if she could get a glimpse of the man from the cave. She was also looking for her daughter whom she hadn't seen all day. The boys who killed the old man entered the village before her; when she reached it they were explaining how they'd slain the old man, displaying the cudgel, which was still wet with blood, beating their chests with delight. Everything began with the fire; people were terrified about the shadows the watchmen had seen. A group of men had cornered the man from up the mountain – the one who had tried to strangle the cement man – and he'd bolted into a house, propped the door shut, and was running along the roof, to see if he could jump from one to another and escape, but they followed him. He told them it wasn't his fault, he'd been blind with rage. The ones on the street called to him to come down, we won't hurt you, come down. The man kept shouting that he wasn't to blame, it was in his blood, while the others continued calling to him to come down. Many hours later the man gave up and came down from the roof. They cracked open his skull, but he wasn't dead, so they strung him up by his feet from a tree in the Plaça. Like a horse, they said, when they left him there; and before returning to the fighting arena, they gave him a shove so he'd swing back and forth. That was when, while the man and my wife . . . yes, that was when the blacksmith's son yanked me by the arm and led me away, I still don't know . . . it all happened so fast, time has muddled everything. When we left the village we came across Senyor's stretcher, abandoned in the open, and the blacksmith's son told me to move fast. A cloud of smoke was pouring out of the stables, followed immediately by flames, and as the flames battled the smoke and wind, the sound of galloping horses reached us. They sped past, almost brushing against us, knocking over the stretcher and Senyor, treading on them. The earth shook, and I covered my ears. When the horses had passed, the blacksmith's son pulled me along and, without knowing how, we found ourselves at Pedres Baixes. Night was ending, and the smell of fire pervaded everything, cleansing it all. Sparks were shooting up from the blacksmith's house, and his son calmly said, that's it. He told me my child was dead. He said, come and you'll see her. He led me to the cemetery on Maraldina. Though still dark, night was ending, and the light from the fires couldn't reach us there. He directed me to the first heather shrubs, where the path began; she was lying there, on her side. I picked her up. Her legs were drawn against her chest. She was on her side. I picked her up and carried her home, leaving her on top of the table. Without saying a word, the blacksmith's son had followed us.

The blacksmith did not want me to entomb my child in the tree. He said he would use the ring for some other dead person. I left home, carrying my child, who had turned wooden, like the table. My innards were on fire, as if the night fire blazed within me. I made my way through a group of men, most of them coming from the blacksmith's. One of them had killed another man by twisting the bones that supported his head. They walked slowly, taking up a lot of room, as if the street were too narrow for them. After they had passed, I looked back at them; they walked like the dead, stiff and stretched tight. Smoke still billowed from the crumpled houses, destroyed by the fire. Some horses stood motionless near the wash area, their reflections doubling them in the water. Many had run away, but others were caught and returned to the enclosure. I had stopped at Pedres Baixes, exhausted, my child in my arms, when the blacksmith's son approached, eyes brilliant and skin that overnight seemed to have grown tight and fresh. The blacksmith's son stopped in front of me, ran his finger across my child's cheek, and said he had seen her leave the village with the boys chasing her, calling out, deformed, deformed. He knew nothing more about her until, on his way back from the stables, a little boy told him she had run away desperately, trying to escape the men who were fighting. As soon as she had left the village she wanted to return, but they had surrounded her; to keep from feeling cornered she had run from one side to the other, all of them pursuing her, shouting. Halfway into town, one had thrown a stone at her, the others followed; all of them threw stones and handfuls of dirt as they corralled her, shouting, go with the dead, with the dead. When they had almost reached the cemetery, they came to a halt, and she turned and faced them. They were silent for a moment, but soon the shouts began. Then a boy picked up a large rock that one of the smaller boys standing next to him was holding and threw it furiously. The rock struck my child on the forehead, and she fell backwards; then they all threw themselves on her and killed her with the rocks. She didn't feel a thing because the first rock left her in a daze. I asked him to tell me which little boy had told him about my child's death. The black-smith's son sat down next to me and told me he would recognize him if he saw him, but he couldn't tell me who it was, he didn't think he had ever seen him before. I could feel the weight of my child on my lap, and there was barely a thread of life left in me. Not because she was dead, but because everything had happened without my understanding it. When she was born, I had not loved her. She looked peculiar when my wife showed her to me; it was as if a nuisance had settled into the house. I wanted to run away, so I would not have to see the thing that clearly I had made, because life is sad, to be born is sad. I could not look at her; everything had turned bitter, less full of life. Her eyes, her legs, every little bit of the flesh I had made – had been made from me – all of it drove me mad. When she cried, I was the one who wished to cry loudly; I would have preferred her not to be born, because I knew what awaited her. Breathing. Only the chore and sadness of breathing and breathing, as things change from tender to dry, new to old, the night-moon that grows thin then swells, the fireless sun that lights up, the soughing of wind that transports, shatters, gathers, and drives away the clouds, raising and flattening the dust. Only the sorrow of going to sleep and waking up, feeling life without knowing where it comes from, aware that it will flee without knowing why it was given to you, why it is taken from you. Here you are: there is this and this and this. And now, enough. I saw the blacksmith's son approaching; I had not noticed that he had left. He was carrying a shovel and he said, it's to dig a hole. Time to go. I stood up, cradling my child in my arms, all of my body still aching from the beating and from lying on the ground during the night. The blacksmith's son carried the shovel. We reached the foot of Maraldina, and I laid my child on the ground, her legs contracted the way I had found her, shriveled up by death; I picked up the shovel and told the blacksmith's son to leave. He said he would help me, but I told him to leave. It was difficult to dig a hole, not because the earth was hard – which it wasn't, just full of little stones – but because I picked up only a bit of dirt with each shovelful. It was taking forever, and the sharp edge of the shovel was digging into my sole from pressing my foot down so often. I wasn't sure if I was making the hole slowly because the shovel removed only a little earth each time, or because the center of my foot hurt, or because as long as the digging lasted I had my child near me and could look at her while I was digging the hole. Let the moment last. But the hole was dug: the same size as my child with shriveled legs. I sat on the ground in front of the hole. A strong, earthy smell reached me, I laid my child in it, on her side because of her shriveled legs. Quiet, alone with my child, amongst the smell of earth and little stones, I again saw the forest and remembered the first day the blacksmith's son had jumped in front of me while my child was sleeping, tired from holding on to my neck as we crossed the river. I had half closed my eyes, the back of my head resting against a tree trunk while at my feet by fits and starts a butterfly was being born, struggling without knowing if it would issue forth, out of itself, like a flower thrusting up from a branch. While I was watching my sleeping child and the butterfly struggling into life, I glimpsed the starveling legs of the blacksmith's son. That was the first time I saw him in broad daylight. My child woke when she sensed something strange nearby – otherwise, she would have slept longer. The blacksmith's son waited for the butterfly to be born, then immediately gave it to my child, and she laughed and looked at the blacksmith's son while the butterfly flapped its wings, tickling her hand. She laughed and looked at the blacksmith's son, and the two of them laughed. When I had come to love her, the two of them laughed together. I watched them laugh, and it seemed as if I was not present because they laughed and I was quiet. I had only the tree behind me, and I had lost everything, except the tree, I lost everything in that moment with the butterfly in the hand that had never held a butterfly. As I sat silently between two laughs, I cast a shadow on my child's face with my hand, but within me I wanted to kill the blacksmith's son. With all my being. I blocked the fiery sun that had risen and was falling full force onto my child's face. The fiery sun rose, and its light fell across the hole, onto my dead child's face, the child who when alive wanted black night because the blacksmith's son had explained that you could only see them in black night. I watched her dead, as if the sun were forcing me to look at her, as if all the time that had passed previously – all the time I had tried to keep from looking at her – all of it now kept my eyes glued to her face. Lying face up, her body on its side. When she was on the verge of dying, she must have looked up. What I saw then is difficult to explain. Her mouth seemed to laugh; a half-open eye was shining, seemingly laughing too. It was the laugh of an elderly person, tired of life, who with a little laugh hides everything. It also seemed like a laugh that was laughing at me, as if it also wanted to convince me that everything I had believed was a lie, that in life, only this was true: the laughter of having been able to die. I threw a shovelful of dirt mixed with stones on her. Then another. And another. I stopped and put down the shovel because my hands suddenly wanted to touch my dead child, from deep inside me I wanted to stroke her. If I had not touched her, I would have thought that she was alive, only playing dead so I would search for her in some place, some hiding place where she was still alive. Her face, her cheek . . . she is not . . . Her legs were dead. I do not know how to say it, I do not know. Her fingers were closed; I took her hand and tried several times to pry open a finger. I did not even realize it was my child's hand, so obsessed was I with trying to make it be the hand I had known: flat, fingers extended, like a hand floating in water that will not harm you. Her little fingers were strong, because they were dead and mine alive. I threw more dirt on her, I had started by throwing dirt on her feet, then moving up to her glassy eyes and mouth. Open your mouth, I would say to her when she was just beginning to understand, and she would open her mouth. I could see the streaked roof of her mouth and the little uvula that would not stop moving. I put down the shovel, feeling there was something I should do, but I was not sure what. Without knowing why, I walked over to Pedres Baixes and returned with a smooth, flat rock that I placed over her head. I covered her with dirt, but her hands showed, especially that one, a bit of skin with a tiny black worm curling and uncurling. Her blood is corrupt. The hand melts away, only the black speck remains. Her hand returns as if wanting to slip beneath the black speck. The knot on her little finger is wrinkled when her hand is open, and when her hand is closed it shines. The hand approaches. Sometimes, when I want it to approach it does not, or it comes with an open hand holding a tremulous butterfly in its palm, and the blacksmith's son releases his fingers from round the butterfly on that first day we met in the forest and they laughed. The hand is dissolving, only a tip remains, a smudge that has been erased, and it too disappears. I finished covering my child with dirt and that first day, first moment, first night, returned to me. Always the first day and first night and the last day and final night, the earth above my dead child forming a mound because the body was a nuisance to the earth, the grave could not hold all of the earth. Using the shovel, I leveled the earth with a few blows and thought that when the village had buried all of its dead, I would place a circle of pebbles on top that would represent a soap bubble, and I would nail the cane she used to make the bubbles in the courtyard into the earth. I knew that time and rain would level the mound, the flesh would dissolve and the earth would settle and above no trace would remain. The pebble circle would come undone, scattered by the rain. Drenched. The bones. Dead bones that are of no use. Better for it all to disappear. No child lies there. Nothing that once breathed. Bones last and last, like stones, like things. The smell of turned-up earth filled everything, the sun had fled, and slender clouds had arrived, letting a fine rain fall, more like dew than rain. Very fine. Rather than being born from grass, it fell from a higher grass, planted far above. I raised my head and opened my mouth, and the thin rain led me to close my eyes. I closed them on purpose so the rain could stroke them and enter my mouth. I held out my palm, still warm from the shovel handle, and waited for each drop of rain as if it were a surprise. Is this it? Yes. That bit of rain falling from a passing cloud that had been rent by the sun, giving rise to the strong odor of recently-moved earth, earth that is not accustomed to air or light, furious that it has been brought to the surface. It was this. Insignificant. Just a trace of life. Now I know. It has been a difficult lesson. It was this thing that comes but never when I want it to, if only again to have a short while, the length of time for a breath or for death, not memory. Memory is worthless. It is. A soft rain one morning at the foot of Maraldina seems like dew that has fallen from I know not what grasses on the summit.

Part Four

I

Many people accompanied me as I prepared to swim under the
village. I don't know who they were; I don't know if we hurried
or dawdled, if they talked or were silent. If I try to recall walking
to the wash area, I cannot. I remember turning back and seeing
the two women from Font de la Jonquilla in the doorway of the
last house in the village, the one with the protruding eyes and the
one with the long braid. I remember the sound of water. I don't
know whether it was because of the women or the sound of the
river, but I thought about two types of water. One good, one bad.
They all wanted it. They had contrived to do it. They were bored
and needed it to keep living. Everyone's face bespoke a craving,
although what they wished was not really clear to them; they just
wished it at whatever cost. I never realized they had all joined
together to do this to me: men, women – even the pregnant
women – the old men from the slaughterhouse, the man in charge
of blood, the faceless men, all of them incited by the blacksmith.
The Festa was late that year because of the fighting and because
the villagers needed time to lick their wounds. I remember the
heat, appearing suddenly out of nowhere, I can still feel it, and the
strong light that was like a summer light when summer blinds. It
returns and furrows into the unease of now, which isn't really
unease, I don't know what it is. The heat beats against the rose-
colored walls of the houses and reflects onto me, blinding me. I
think endlessly about my life and feel that it is dying. The broad
river flowed past, covering the banks, flattening the grass. It carried away earth and stones whose edges had been polished by the
years. Joyful mornings still exist, but where I can't say. Amidst the
canes, perhaps, in the wind rustling through leaves, in the wing
feathers of mourners as they circle Muntanyes Morades but never

venture to Maraldina. Everyone was in the Plaça. Dark smudges marked the tree – and the ground beneath it – where the man had hung by his feet for three days. The two old men who held up the stake-laden trunk seemed wooden, their fingers full of tree nodes rather than knots. I should have told them to leave, or grabbed them by the collar and choked them. It seemed like years since the day I took my child to Font de la Jonquilla, but in reality only a short time had passed. My life had been filled with the struggle of growing, the kind of death my father endured, everything he did to me, everything that happened round me. Life had turned ugly from so much living. This never-ending chain of men and women coming together, children never ceasing to be born. My mother had been beautiful, and then one day, without knowing what had happened, she turned ugly. Everyone was in the Plaça, and the race had finished. The moment had come to swim the river. I looked up. The window in Senyor's house was closed; the ivy was sending up sprouts that stretched upward as far as the windowsill. The pregnant women, with only the lower part of their faces showing, were sitting in the Plaça under the shade of the trees. My wife had climbed up on a branch and was observing it all as she swung her hard-soled feet back and forth high above the ground. The blacksmith's son had spent hours lying on the spot where the prisoner's cage had stood. The aftermath of the clash was apparent: fewer men in the village, dark smudges on the tree, burnt houses being rebuilt.

When I drew the forked stick, which was practically placed in my hand, the pregnant women raised their heads and laughed out of the corners of their mouths. While still in the Plaça, an old man said, drink. The drink they forced on me burnt my throat, my entire body, as it went down. The blacksmith came over to me, slapped me on the back a few times and said, don't be afraid. I don't know who accompanied me. I can visualize the two women from Font de la Jonquilla standing motionless, their eyes fixed on me; for a long time I could feel their gaze on my back, at once a burden and a companion. I remember the blacksmith; he was with the others who accompanied me. He walked beside me. A child holding a cane appeared out of nowhere and drew a line on the ground, shouting with his hands in the air that we couldn't cross it. We stepped on it, the broken line through which things escape when you are little, broken from within, the break through which everything escapes. I can't see the blacksmith, but I see his mouth – lips the color of crimson powder, teeth rotten, eyes that never looked but always saw. The child who had drawn the line was standing in the middle of the street; I saw him again the last time I turned round. We reached the river, right at water level. I didn't strip. I approached the edge of the river without knowing why I was there. My mouth filled with the strong taste of the drink, a wave of blood in my forehead, throbbing and throbbing. The blacksmith removed my clothes. I'll have to take care of you . . . He took my clothes off slowly, blocking the sun . . . Standing beside the water, my back to everyone, I felt as if I were more insignificant than the thing I was before I was born. A large hand gave me a shove on the head. Before I fell into the water, I had a glimpse of the blacksmith's son facing me from the other side of the river.

II

I felt as if I was water and my body of flesh and bones had stayed on land with my clothes. The water pulled me under. As I had neither hands nor legs, at first the water drew me down. The drink did not calm my fear: it numbed my arms and legs. When I emerged from the glass darkness, I still carried the afternoon glare with me and I could see nothing. Then the shadows split; just as I felt that all was lost, a rock stopped me. I grabbed hold of it and my legs and arms seemed to come alive again. It occurred to me that perhaps the drink only numbed you at the beginning. I caught the strong smell of moss, and the rock beneath my hand was viscous, snot-like. My father's hand was large, covered with hairs, the dry skin cracked, a white half-moon at the base of his fingernails. When I was little my father was a hand. A hand behind my head, pushing me forward, grow up fast, you're a nuisance. If I was in the dining room, he pushed me into the courtyard; if I was in the courtyard, he pushed me toward the dining room. My mother said my father was changing, becoming strange. He would leave and we wouldn't see him for two or three days. He would return and act like he always had, but he stayed away longer each time. That's when my mother began her plaintive keening beneath the windows of newlyweds. She grew full of rage, sometimes whimpering and groaning, we won't ever see him again. He always returned, but I fretted over the idea that he might not, and I would sit and listen behind the door, my back nailed to the wood. In the end, every time my father reappeared, my mother would tell him that it would be better if he never came back. Let him leave and not come back, let him leave and not come back. My back to the door, sleepless, listening to the sounds from the street, I would whisper in a low voice, don't come back, don't come back. He started saying he wanted to kill himself, he was going to kill himself and we would never see him again, one day we would wait for him and never see him again. He looked at us and said he would kill himself, and when he killed himself he would laugh thinking we would be waiting for him but would never again see him. And then my mother grew ugly. The water was freezing. With the hand that wasn't holding tight, I touched the rock. At first I was repulsed, but then I liked it; I could feel it against my back, darkness streaming out of the rock. He would say, in order to survive, you have to live as if you are dead. He said it as if he weren't addressing anyone, while my stepmother sat on top of the table stringing flowers, one after the other. When my stepmother first came home with us, she began to change and my mother said . . . No, that was before my stepmother arrived, when my father first began to say he wanted to kill himself. When my stepmother appeared, my mother was already dead, I think. Yes, my mother was already dead. I realized during the early days with my stepmother that father had changed; he was the man he had been years before: he would come home happy, his eyes glowing. Later, his face always showed the same thing. It never changed, and he entered the house slowly. When my mother died, he told me that in order to survive you have to live as if you are dead. The following day I crossed the river with the bee chasing me; I wanted to visit the tree cemetery I had never seen. My father had grown thin; he said he couldn't sleep, on certain nights the lifeless gash on his forehead seemed alive. He had grown thin and the tree was consuming him, as darkness was consuming me. I rubbed my hand over the slimy rock, again and again. The water created fat waves against the rock and I swayed back and forth. I felt there was no time; Time, I mean, was not present. It merely created light and change. I wanted to move, wanted to cross to the other side of the rock to see if . . . And while I was thinking about the 'if,' a huge wave crashed against me and swept me away. Like a tiny particle I floated downstream until something blocked me and my feet got entangled. The smell of moss was settling in my nose, stronger than before. I wanted to disengage my feet from the reeds, but I couldn't. The harder I tried to loosen them, the stronger they clasped me. Something horrible grew in my chest, as if a lump that held the fear of life, fear of people, fear of the unknown had formed in the center of my chest. A lump filled with suffering in the center of my chest, secured by root-like nerves. The reeds were binding me tighter and tighter. Like rope. She had told me to make a rope for her. The first winter she was with us. I ignored her. But when my father was dead and I slept at the foot of her door so I could hear her breathing . . . The river flowed through my bound feet as it circled the earth like a snake wanting to bite its tail. She made me enter the room where she slept with my father. No, my father was already dead. She opened a box and pulled out a rope, saying it was very old, tomorrow you'll make me a new one. Two of them, many of them. She gave me some hemp and told me I had to make more rope: thin, fat, a lot of rope. Rolled up inside the box, the rope I made her looked like a young snake on top of an old snake. Beneath it lay the rope that was her mother and the awl that was used on me when I was little. When we were going to have the child, she clawed me, made my cheek bleed, told me that no one had ever made her a child. When she heard me enter the house, she hid; if I called to her, she fled and sometimes didn't come back all night. She would go and watch the man with the cudgel fighting with the village boys. She would watch from her hiding place, hear the shrill sound he made with his tongue, the things he said and she couldn't understand. When the old man entered the cave, leaving a boy lying unconscious on the ground, she would come out of her hiding place in the grass and kick the boy in the ribs. My legs were trapped, and I was enveloped by darkness, the whole village above me, a group of men waiting for me to emerge. I would have stayed there, among the reeds, with the cold water. I was thirsty and sick. I drank some water and was thirstier still because the thirst was born deep within me, beneath the lump in my chest, and the water couldn't reach it. My tongue was thick; the taste from the drink had grown stronger, and my mouth was salty and sour. I ran my tongue over my teeth, finding everywhere the taste that grew and grew, changing from salty and sour to bitter. I touched my teeth and glassy eyes without understanding that I was doing it. As if, without my realizing, some other person wanted to touch my eyes to see if the slime was on my teeth, in my eyes, on the rocks dashed by the water as it surged from inside the earth. Darkness emerged thick, as if night – the night I carried within me, that no one could dislodge – were gushing from the rocks. I moved a leg, and the reeds that bound me seemed less strong. I grabbed hold of something and leaned down, how cold, and severed many of the reeds, some were stubborn, some decomposing. Little by little, I constructed a well of water without reeds around me, and when I was on the verge of being able to escape from that prison, I didn't. I saw my child and the blacksmith's son. I saw them the first time I crossed the river, not alone but with my child in the patch of dog roses, spider webs stuck to her leg, she had said, get it off, get it off . . . you knew it, you knew it, you knew it. With an effort I disentangled myself from the reeds, though some of them still wished to grasp me. Again, Time, and no way of knowing if I had been among the reeds very long, the water and me beneath the village, all of me on fire, the cold water carrying me along. I stretched out an arm and found a branch to clasp, it was a root, coming from above, the roots that upwrenched houses were dry, and some, wishing to drink, had come in search of the water that flowed beneath them. I tightened my hand round the root, as if it were a friend, as if it were the prisoner's hand waiting for me ever since that night because he had been able to escape his suffering when I had shouted that the village was burning. I felt my head becoming clearer; I was again becoming me, with arms and legs that could swim and walk. Everything was darker near the root. Darker than all the darkness I had left behind. The rock wall was slimy, the moss grass-like; I followed the course of the water with my hands as it combed the moss, flattening it. This rock was slimier than the other, as if all the snails, all the slugs had deposited their mucus and foam on it. The rock was a snakeskin, and snake and water were one and the same, and the river of the dead killed whoever swam beneath the village . . . As if suddenly awakening, I felt an obstacle approaching. An obstacle and an odor. I stopped breathing, as if the thing lived only in my head, as if I could kill it by holding my breath. It and the smell were approaching, closer and closer. I glimpsed a darker shadow within the blackness and a faint gleam. Out of fear of the thing approaching with its breath, I loosened my grasp on the root, and the water swept me away, leaving the malodor behind; again, I found my arms and legs numb. I cried out, as if someone could hear me and come to my aid. I was alone, and the rock crushed my forehead, many sharp-edged rocks slashing me at the same time. The whole ceiling had lowered, water and ceiling meeting, or the river had risen. A mouthful of water was mixed with the taste of blood. The water deposited me on top of a rock. Whether I rested there for a short time or longer, life had ended. My innards burned, and I was sur-rounded by freezing water. I could hear water surging, a waterfall, I thought. Only water, the flowing water, and my aching fore-head, everything was moving, the river widening, the ceiling rising as if it were made of resin that the water could erase. I had only to wait. The rock was warm. I was dead, and Time did not exist. I could feel a breath-like warmth entering my body. I moved my hand away and reached toward my sleeping father's mouth, when he breathed out, I moved my hand away, my father had fallen asleep in the courtyard, seated in a chair, early one after-noon. The gash on his head was recent, and I wanted to look at his eyes, know if he could see me through the slit in his eyes, even though he was asleep. I tiptoed over to him, leaned down to gaze into his eyes. He was sleeping, and the bit of eye that was left open was staring. I placed my open hand in front of his eyes. He didn't budge. He seemed to see me, but didn't. He was breathing deeply, and a rattle rose from his throat. I waved my open palm before his eyes, then held my hand in front of his mouth; his breath was warm as it came and went. One night, shortly thereafter, I saw . . .

I saw it in my sleep but I was awake, on the real day, in the court-yard, there was a green brightness, and my mother's blue apron lay on the table, and that night I noticed that the light in the court-yard was also green and the apron on the table, blue. Afternoon and night merged. My father was reclining in the same chair in the center of the courtyard, but fog circled his feet, round his legs. I wanted to look at his eyes. I was just as frightened as that after-noon. Frightened that he might see me, frightened he might wake up. Again, I waved my hand before his eyes, he didn't seem to see me, even though the slit in his eye was shining. When I was tired of leaning over to look in his eyes, I placed my open hand in front of his mouth, and while I was doing that, I thought about the fog that enveloped his legs, but I didn't dare look at it. I was thinking about the fog when I had to jerk my hand away because the breath escaping my father's mouth was fiery hot. I glanced down at my stinging palm. It was scarlet and large, like the palms of the man with the cudgel; I backed away, but my father's burning breath still reached me, like a scorching wind. I kept changing places, moving about the courtyard, my father's chair spinning round as if its four legs were not fixed to the ground, his breath following me, hotter and hotter. I don't know how I managed to get to the dining room; from there everything seemed far away. I went upstairs and lay on the bed, my heart pounding. I shut the door. I think I was falling asleep, I don't remember a thing. I couldn't see the door because it was at the head of the bed. I couldn't see it. Without seeing the door, which lay just behind my head, I observed a ring of fire in front of me, at the foot of the bed. Ember red. A black ring began to form near it. The smell of burning wood didn't reach me until the black ring had formed. I was un-able to think why I was seeing what I was seeing and shouldn't be. A hole formed in the center of the embers, and the embers closest to the hole were surrounded by ashes. As the black ring widened, the embers followed it and the hole grew larger. My father's mouth appeared in the center of the hole, his breath burning the door. When I realized that the door behind me now lay before me, at the foot of the bed, and that my father would begin to burn me, a rattle rose in my throat, the rattle my father had that afternoon in the courtyard. I awoke then, sweating and trembling. I couldn't keep my hands from shaking or a knot from quickly swelling on my upper arm, as if an animal were living beneath my skin. The stone was warm, like breath. Wanting to know how large the stone was, I tried extending my leg to see if I could reach the edge of it with the tip of my foot, but it was as if I had no legs, only a swelling. The stone was warm, as if a calm stream of hot water were emerging from it. Slimy against my cheek. For a time that was not time, I lay with the cold and heat, a rattle in my throat, on top of the rock, as if I had turned to rock . . . I looked round and when I wanted to shut my eyes, I couldn't. During that time when Time did not exist, the pain in my forehead had grown, and groans issued from my mouth of their own accord. I would have liked to touch my pain, know what had happened to my forehead, but I could not raise my arm, and I flattened myself against the rock. I would have stayed there forever, but just as the water had deposited me there, it carried me away. More furious, more enraged, the real thing. It swept me up, swept me away, and when the ceiling was almost upon me, I felt another low ceiling approaching, like the one that had reached down to the water and, again, the water forced me upward, as if offering me to the rock. I felt my forehead being ripped away. My entire forehead. The healed wound on my father's forehead looked like blood when he raged or when it was very hot. It ripped his forehead off, someone was saying in a low voice as she nursed me.

III

The glare was so terrible when they removed the bandages from my eyes that I wanted to shut them but couldn't. I covered them with my arm. An old woman, one of the group who had shouted horrid words at Senyor, told me that fire had consumed my body the first days after swimming under the village; she said I had talked about the prisoner. I put my hand to my forehead; I was missing an eyebrow. The old woman looked at me calmly, her hands clasped together over her stomach, and told me not to touch the wound because the skin was still very tender. She was small, with sunken cheeks, her earth-colored skin furrowed with deep wrinkles that went from her eyes all the way to the bottom of her face. She stared at me with an open mouth. My legs almost gave out when I stood up; instinctively I headed toward the village, and as I walked, my legs again learnt how to walk. I left without saying a word to the old woman who had taken care of me. At the entrance to the village, I turned back and headed to the stables. The enclosure had been rebuilt, reinforced. But the stables were just as they were the night of the fire. I remember stopping at the Festa esplanade. With the glare, everything looked blurred. A man walking in the distance seemed to be a man who lived only in my thoughts, and my thoughts could not bring him into focus. I reached the part of the river where calm water joined it. The canes were still. I sighted the tree of death on Maraldina. To my left, farther away, lay the dark green smudge of the forest of the dead with the higher mountains beyond, rising one behind the other. I sat down on a bench, my head on my arms, my arms on the table. I looked at my feet, moved them, scattered a bit of earth, then suddenly I kicked the ground and struck the table. I stood up, holding my arm in front of my eyes, and edged toward the canes in the water. Dead leaves and brush were floating on the river and a piece of driftwood where the canes started. In the shady spots, the green water looked black. I leaned down to the water, letting half of my body hang over it. I rested on my hands and knees: head over the river, body over the shore, hands in the mud. I remained like that for a while, gazing in front of me at the other side of the river; then I looked down into the water and saw my father's face.

It was dark when I got home. The door was open and my wife was standing at the entrance to the courtyard. I stood before her, but she wouldn't look at me. When she finally did, she turned her back. I left the village in the early morning and didn't stop until I reached the spot where they had thrown me in the river. The sky was beginning to turn pink. The blacksmith's son was lying down; from a distance I couldn't tell if he was sleeping or if he could see me. I returned to the village. The men leaving their houses passed by me, but it was as if they had not passed anyone. They talked among themselves, said 'bon dia' to each other, as if I were a shadow, nothing at all. That night I went round to the blacksmith's son. He told me I didn't need to visit him, he didn't need anyone. Said he spent all his time thinking about the fire, the joy of setting fire to the stables and his house, his father's house. Said he wasn't the one who set fire to the other houses. It all began when the boys returned from killing the old man with the cudgel, but he had been responsible for the killing because he had made people realize that without his cudgel the man was less than a feeble old woman. If he hadn't hidden the cudgel that night, the old man would still be alive. I who have always seemed dead, I killed half the village. As he gazed at his blazing house, he had felt something he couldn't explain, as if he were master of it all. He could give everyone orders, see them all bowing to him, subservient. Some were throwing water on the fire, others crushing the old man's head, fire and flames spitting into the air, causing the black night to glimmer. I – he said, speaking in a clear voice – I who have spent all my life in bed, without food, I was in charge. My father – his legs crooked, his nails black from working with iron – was running back and forth, unable to cage the prisoner. Now I have made myself a prisoner, and I won't stop until I am confined in the cage. The whole village will say the blacksmith is an evil man who caged his own son. He drew near me, looked at my face, and said, they made you a face like your father's. Better that your child be dead, that she not see you with this face that isn't a face, a child who was everyone's child, you knew she was everyone's child. You've always been subservient, you who could eat according to your appetite and I, son of the blacksmith, always ill, I set fire to my father's house, I was in charge for one whole night. Man is partly from air, partly from earth – the prisoner's stories – he always told the same, but it was the blacksmith's son who set fire to the village, and the villagers still think the clash began because some of them wanted people entombed with cement, others without. All that was needed was to set the village on fire while their minds were on other things. We will never have another man with a cudgel, but we will have a prisoner. My father won't have the house he once had; everything that I had wished for as I lay in bed had seeped into the walls and died with them. He asked me to touch him, so I would see he was alive. He said he wouldn't die for some time yet, in order to remember that night when he roamed the village filled with joy, more joy than he was able to express, while all the men fought each other. Don't think about it; you have to believe that it's all the same to have a face or have your forehead ripped away. It's all the same to live or die if you have to live as I was made to live. Learn to make fire by rubbing sticks together; learn to start a fire and you'll be happy. A fire that causes damage.

I remembered a little animal with four legs and a tail that had allowed itself to be caught because I pretended I hadn't seen it. When it had calmed down, I picked it up by its soft belly; its eyes bulged from its head. That animal came to mind because I felt as if I was being followed by several people, not just one, but the sound of the waterfall prevented me from hearing their footsteps clearly.

I heard them when a branch broke, then another snapped. In the village, people pretended they didn't see me, weren't aware of me, as if I were dead, more than dead, so they could enjoy hunting me down, make my eyes bulge. The animal's eyes were honey-colored. Without knowing where I wanted to go that night, I had headed to Font de la Jonquilla; I could see the tall shadow of the mountain in front of me, to my left the river and the trees I had loved when I was little, the ones that swayed in the wind – the entire tree, root to tip – and stretched upward during the night. I turned round sharply when the branch broke and again when it snapped. As the branch snapped, I thought I saw a shadow hiding behind a tree trunk. Everything that was green and leafy grew during the night, not with sun and light, but secretly, during the night. I too hid behind a tree trunk and waited there for a moment, but I heard nothing. Only the waterfall and the sound of gushing water. In the moonless night the river was black, and the path gradually turned away from the river as it approached Font de la Jonquilla. Again, I hid from the shadow walking behind me. As it passed me, I thought it looked like my wife, who no longer lived at home. I covered my eyes with my arm. After a while I started walking again. Someone was at Font de la Jonquilla, so I climbed to the spot where the white-flowered ivy grew and curled up. Not even the tree trunks were visible; everything was silent except the faint sound of the waterfall and the nearby fountain splashing over the rocks. The air was cool and the ivy leaves rustled, brushing against each other, giving the impression of speaking to one another every time they touched. Very close to me I heard someone move. Or were there two of them? Everything was dark. It seemed to be turning darker and darker, as if darkness were growing, emerging from the leaves that brushed each other. The smell of water and flowers reached me. The sound of gushing water from the fountain broke off for a moment, and I assumed someone was drinking from cupped hands. Then I heard the water cascading again with full force. I listened and heard someone groaning, but not from pain, and the groans were mixed with the sound of the water. I left my hiding place and jumped down, not sure where I had landed, but I could sense the shadow. I couldn't see it, but I could feel it and the cool air from the water blowing through my toes. Then the shadow jumped on me, grabbed me by the neck, and was tightening its grip on me, but I was able to throw it off and ran as fast as I could, somehow finding the path that led away from the fountain. The shadow chased me, but I ran faster, until finally I was back at the river and trees and the shadow came to a halt. It wasn't the same shadow that had followed me at the beginning. I heard it turn back toward the fountain, and gradually the sound of the waterfall grew fainter, until it finally melted away, and only the noise of the river by the growing trees remained. The shadow's breath smelled of dead horse.

IV

I wandered about during the night. I couldn't sleep, and I roamed the night and came to understand why my father had done what he did and to understand better what lay ahead of me, but I can't explain it. A few days after the night at Font de la Jonquilla, I fled, more from my face than from the village. It hurt if the children chased me during the day crying, his wife's left him, but it hurt much more for them to see my ravaged face, and because my face was ravaged, they shouted what they did about my wife leaving me. Perhaps my hideous face was the real one, the one I should have had all along, but I couldn't recognize myself in it; I was another, I was my father, and when I entered the house, I found it empty because my wife had returned to the old men at the slaughterhouse, where she had lived when she was little, before the shadow took my father, his life and all. More than anyone else, I carry the village inside me, from my night wanderings. I couldn't lose my way even with my eyes blindfolded. Little by little everything had become different, obliterated, broken. Things become effaced, as if after great suffering the hurt seems distant, the pain far away, so distant that it becomes more bearable. In black night, standing in the moonlight on top of the stone clock, I was Time. The moon gazing at me. Time moved forward with difficulty, and as I stood there, something fled from within me, from the hour, from Time. The thing that fled from me floated above the river, near the canes, observing the movement of the water. I looked to see if rings were forming in the water. I thought they were, but they weren't. Standing on top of the sundial stone, the circles I wanted to see were the ones from that morning, made by a hand I never saw again. I was lost between two different hours, always waiting for what was to come, drawing circles in the air with my hand, but they didn't spread like the ones in the water; I couldn't make them appear, no matter how much I waved my hand. I could see only the shadow of my arm – which didn't seem like mine – and the shadow of my body cast on the stone. Little by little, everything melted away, and the thing that had fled from within me was returned to me, devalued. I headed toward the village, slowly following the empty streets, smelling the last remnants of spring in the wisteria leaves, the vanishing spring that had lost its way. In black night I searched the streets for the girl, and if I heard the faceless men coming, I hurried to another street. If I thought she lived on the street where I was walking, a sickly respite entered my heart, but it was only a brief respite because I would again wish to flee, wish not to be seen. Every time I stepped down from the sundial stone, I thought that would be the night I would find her. A glimmer of light was beginning to appear behind me, rising from Pedres Altes. I returned to the village later every night, not that I didn't want to return, but because I lacked the will to want. One night I went to the esplanade. I collected clay, and without knowing what I was doing, I made a little figure. The clay was too soft and the figure doubled over; I made two legs for it, but they buckled when they were joined to the body. In the distance I heard a horse neigh; it was coming from the wash area. The air echoed with the neighing that issued from the blacksmith's son, the same neighing heard that night in the center of the village. I broke off a twig and pierced the figure, running the twig lengthwise through the center of the body, up to the head, then I shaped an arm. I also pierced the soles of the tiny feet with twigs and pushed them up the legs. I gazed at the still soft figure and, holding it in the middle, moved it forward, its feet resting on the ground. It looked as if it were walking. Sometimes I would lift it up a bit and let it fall toward the water. It was neither person nor bird. I made a lot of them, left them all facing the water. I enjoyed thinking of the rings spreading in the water that morning, maybe they were somewhere out of sight. The day after I moulded the figure, I didn't go to the sundial. I was drawn to the esplanade, as if the figure I had left lying on the ground was calling to me. I went there every night, slept there, and in the morning, as if a hand were shaking my shoulder, I awoke. I gathered twigs, tied them together with leaf veins and covered them with clay. I formed tiny bones, fastened them securely, then covered them with clay, legs and all, the back too. I moulded many tiny figures with only one arm; I fashioned my child, my children, and while I was making them, I would think about my wife living with the old men and going to Font de la Jonquilla at night. I didn't care that she went there. I made a larger figure that was my wife, so she would be with me. I threw it in the water soon after making it, because she was no longer the person who had been with my father, or the person who had been with me. She said she left me because I had become like my father and dead people frightened her. When she told me, she made the same face she did the day she told me she didn't love our child, she just didn't; she hadn't wanted her, the child had arrived without being asked, settling into the house, carving out a space within the air where my wife lived. A sense of unease had settled on me because of my child's life, because she would have to breathe without knowing why, without understanding why the light changed colors or the wind its course. I had felt like crying for my deformed child who was only the beginnings of a person. Her eyes shone, but she still couldn't talk. She would follow the direction of my arm, linking word to object. That's how she learned to say leaf. I would pronounce the word for her, then pick up a leaf as I mouthed it.

The figures waited for me. The broken ones I remade, and with soft clay I filled the crevices of the ones that had cracked. I modeled figures with arms and made them walk while they were still quite soft. I would stand one on the ground, an arm extended toward me, and step back. Sometimes I had to put clay round the figure to prop it up, and I would brush the fingertips, which were just a handful of clay, with my finger; I didn't know how to fashion fingers, and if I tried, they always fell off. I would pick up the figure and draw it close to my neck and cheek. There was no sign of affection. Affection means skin brushing against skin; it may seem like nothing at all, but the pulsing of blood was shared. The girl from the river was nowhere to be seen. If she was nearby and had seen me, she would have fled – like my wife – her disheveled hair, her hands and feet. Perhaps the only thing that would remain of her would be the marks her wet feet made on the ground as she fled. Those feet carried something warm and tender above them that would have helped me to live and sleep and breathe.

With the break of day, I saw death. I was death reflecting in the water the face of a dead person. I didn't know why I thought that. Where does death begin? I asked myself. Did it spring from your skin or surface from beneath it? Was it at your fingertips, at that point in your entrails where the pain of life begins, at your elbow, in the center of your knee? Where did it begin to kill? Where did each person's death reside? In sleep or in the awakening? Did death die tired from having killed? When skin turned cold, flesh hardened, and all grew icy and wooden, where had death gone? If death was each person and each person was death, why don't we refer to 'deaths'? The deaths of men and women, deaths waiting inside like the worms of misery. The deaths of children: silent, hidden, ready for the stone to strike. One eye open and laughing. Why not 'deaths are coming,' instead of 'death is approaching.' Deaths inside trees. Arborideaths – rotted from within – die in the end. The tree that has sheltered death turns very slowly to dust, over time's time. It comes apart. It is like a caterpillar, the prisoner had said. Death lives within the tree, like the butterfly within the caterpillar. To emerge from within is painful. Many butterflies die when they emerge from the caterpillar; if they are unable to send blood to the wings, they die, caught in the dry caterpillar's skin. Perhaps the soul flees without any color, unable to weep, alone and abandoned. People think it is locked inside by cement, beneath the bark; the prisoner said it escapes, always searching for the point where the flesh comes undone the fastest, where the tree is quick to open. It lives within the tree, from the farthest tip of the last leaf down to the deepest base of the root. The deaths surrounded me, escaped from trees, like flowers furiously strewn far and wide. My death was me, my heart a prisoner to my veins, binding me above and below, at my sides. Like snakes that never spare you, heading to my liver, my breath, arcing as they split in two, so that now the pair of them can be put to use. All of this beneath my ribs. Desire is born and grows strong at the center of the heart. Many mornings, as I was moulding clay figures, I would be short of breath and open my mouth, my hands grasping the air, trying to force it inside me, but it would not enter. I would destroy the figures; I would pick up those I had made with only one arm and crush them. Those with two arms I would gather, one by one, and hold under the water so they would slowly dissolve. The water consumed them in the same way that my father's death was consuming my life. The following day I would again make figures. I wanted a lot of them. A whole village of figures, all the same, two arms, and I would talk to them in a voice so low, so full of sighs, that it wasn't my voice. Tenderness changed me into water and everything that fled from me was in that water. I don't know why, I don't know what those mornings were because no words exist for them. No. No words exist. They have to be invented.

V

I was standing before the river, by the marsh, listening to the night. I thought I saw rings in the water. All my being brought the girl to life, brought her to me, her hair pulled high, and when she was almost at my side, it fell loose, down her back. She drew nearer and melted into me as if she and I were fog. She stepped back and took me by the arm with two strong, tiny hands, and we began to walk, we headed toward the water; as we approached it, the river withdrew, farther and farther away, as we walked. I had never walked with anyone like that. My wife and I would stroll hand in hand, or I would put my arm on her shoulder, or she would hold me by the waist, and it was something children did. But the girl from the water stood very close to me, held my arm with both of her hands and laughed. I couldn't see her face. She didn't have a face, but she laughed. We walked like that for a long time, toward the dead water at the head of the dry, sandy trail that lay before us. Motionless canes forming a fan-like vault sprouted on both sides of the narrow path, and soon the girl and I would walk through them, unable to see sky or mountain, only leaves. She dropped my arm and stood in front of me, I in front of her. Lips at the level of lips, eyes at the level of eyes, hearts troubled, but it was as if only separation existed, as if the two could never meet. I could feel her bird-breath beseeching tenderness. At that moment I stepped back from the unknown, and my voice, not addressing anyone, whispered very softly, don't wish for this.

I reached the marsh. At the edge the mud flower grew, a lone flower born without green leaves. There were patches of them.

From the damp sprouted a new-green stem, topped by a bud. The bud grew large, the green streaked with the color of crimson dust. One day I had curled up, waiting for the flower to blossom. It made a clicking sound when it opened and the flower released the leaves. I plucked it, and bitter, viscous water spurted from the stem. If you touched it and rubbed your fingers over your lips, you got sores. All of a sudden, I realized what I desired: sorrow. The stones scattered in the mud were like sorrow, patches of sorrow. I turned back. I don't know how long I wandered about during those nights. The clay figures were dead, destroyed. I was searching for a bond, but I didn't know what I was searching for or where to look. Now I know, now that my life has come full circle, like a glass ball on the verge of shattering. I waited for dawn to examine myself in the water. With my hand over my mouth, the water reflected grief-filled eyes. The sky was wide, the earth wide, the village small. I clutched a rock, and as if the hand were someone else's, I struck my forehead. My eyes filled with tears, although I had no wish to cry, and I saw everything as if I were under water, but now salty drops filled my eyes. I raised my arm and gazed at my hand; it wasn't the hand I wished. I made my way to the blacksmith's to see his son. He was lying down, touching himself, and I pretended I didn't see him. To avoid seeing him, I thought about hands: my child's, Senyor's, the hands of the old man who had given me the drink. I looked at mine, and the hand didn't belong to anyone, not to me, or the water, or life, or death. The same as me. My hand, like me.

I had to stop at the slaughterhouse. I was ill and paused by the wall to gaze into the distance. Clouds were coming from the direction of Pedres Altes. I glanced up. Looking at the slowly approaching clouds made me dizzy. I turned round, my face to the wall, and banged my forehead against it. I felt like vomiting, but didn't. The stench of dead horse rose from the wall, blending with the night air, attempting to restore past things to life, things that could no longer be, things that wished to live again for a moment but could not. I started walking toward my house, afraid I wouldn't make it. The door was ajar, and I could see a bit of starlight in the courtyard at the end. That's when they beat me. The voice of the person beating me was telling me to stop wandering at night: if I continued to roam about at night, they would kill me. The words carried the stench of dead horse and the memory of swimming under the village. As the river hurled me along, the breath of that thing that had approached me, causing me to release my grip on the root, bore the stench of dead horse, but I hadn't recognize it that day because it was accompanied by the smell of water and moss. It was the same malodor from the shadow that had pursued me at Font de la Jonquilla, the same breath. The blacksmith struck me, again and again, until I turned round and knocked him to the floor. He grabbed my legs, trying to pull me down, but there was a door behind me and I let myself fall against it. When he stood up I kicked him, heard him groan. He must have rolled away because I couldn't find him. Again, he threw himself on me and knocked me senseless.

I woke up feeling I was being watched. I ached all over, like that night by the river while the village went up in flames. They were looking at me. My wife was kneeling in front of me, very close, looking into my eyes, as I had looked into my father's that afternoon in the courtyard. She moved away when I stirred. Seated with my back to the wall, I bent forward, as if I were searching for a link with life, but the feelings that bound me were like blighted grass, and I leaned back against the wall. When my wife left, I stood up not knowing what to do. I opened the white wooden box that had blackened over the years; inside it lay the old rope and awl. I leaned over, gazing for a long time at the rope and awl, until finally my knees began to hurt. Then I picked up the rope, wrapped it round my wrist three times, and with my free hand followed the rope to the end. But I discovered nothing.

Lightning flashed, followed by a clap of thunder. Before the rain began to fall, more thunder sounded, as if the sky were rent and the lightning had come to cauterize the heavenly wounds. The water fell like a torrent over the house. It rained all night, the sky never tiring until early morning.

VI

I wanted to see the village. The wisteria trunk in front of my empty house bore three incisions that my mother had carved. The men were leaving for work, and I looked them in the face. Never before that morning had I gazed so intently at the faces of the people from my village. The men didn't look at me, the women did, but I couldn't discern if the women looked at me with pity or revulsion. The men had dismissed my face from those things that were visible. Old faces, young faces, all of them bear life experiences, as if histories were written on them. Suddenly I could hear a hammer striking the anvil. It was coming from the opposite direction. The last faces were those of three children. I left the village by the stables and headed toward the Pont de Fusta, where three little boys were fighting with sticks. I stopped. Two of them were running about, but one knew how to dodge the blows without moving and strike the others. The one delivering blows had a long, narrow face with little eyes and a low forehead. The other two had round faces, large ears, and desperate eyes. I started across the bridge, but I came to a halt when I reached the center. The day was limpid, the sky and water young, the dark mountains sharply outlined against the sky. The day was so clear I could almost count the trees on the farthest mountains. I retraced my steps. The little boys were still fighting. When they saw I was returning, they stopped fighting for a moment, and I covered my eyes with my arm. One of the round-faced boys came and stood by me, and when I began to walk, he did too. Soon he left me because I was moving slowly. He trudged in front of me, but stayed close by. From time to time he twisted round, searching for my feet, and when he had seen them, he would turn his back to me. At the horse enclosure, I stopped to contemplate Maraldina, the Muntanyes Morades, and Senyor's mountain with the still green ivy. It was tiring to look that far away. In my pocket I carried the awl my mother had used to pierce my ears when I was little. You can have everything you want, but accompanied by pain, until you learn not to want anything. I had found it in the box where my wife kept the ropes. I paused to look at the grazing horses, their coats shiny, eyes entranced. I turned back round and the little boy was standing firmly in front of me, his head up, staring at me. The sun was falling on the esplanade of Pedres Baixes. Behind Pedres Altes it was all grey, everything was lost in the greyness where the watchmen lived with the tiny horses whose tails reached the ground. The little boy continued on his way in front of me, but he turned round from time to time, until we parted at the end of the horse enclosure. When I looked he was far away, and I could barely make out the dead tree on Maraldina because of the curve in the Festa esplanade. When I reached the bend in the river, I searched for the place where I had crossed the first time. I remembered a shrub on the left, but it has disappeared. I knew the shrub was there that day because at first I had planned to leave my clothes beside it rather than by the tree. Many trees were now scattered about the area. Close to the water, I found a spot I didn't remember: long and narrow, covered with large, very white pebbles. Where had I crossed? Memory plays tricks on us. The man who killed the serpent had died at the bend in the river, trampled by his horse; I didn't know it the first time I swam across. He and his horse had been one and the same as they chased the serpent; then they became two. I was looking for some small sign, whatever it was that could help me find where I had crossed. I strolled up and down, occasionally placing my arm in front of my eyes because the light was getting stronger and I couldn't bear the glare. I undressed and sat naked, my back against a tree, feeling the support. To my left, in front of the marsh, lay the mud-flower pond. To my right, at a distance, the canes by the esplanade. The morning was dead, the canes swaying, and in the daylight the green water was almost colorless. Water got in my eyes. Soon the blacksmith's house would be ready, as well as everyone else's; the horses would neigh on moonlit nights and the blacksmith's son would respond and the man would be . . . Water got in my eyes; the river was very broad in that spot. Calm, but very broad. Shiny flecks on the sun-splashed water, darkly mottled where there was no sun. When I got out, I sat down to rest. I would have wished for things to come, but things did not come. The grasses were breathing, enjoying the moment; I was breathing only from exhaustion, having swum the breadth of the river.

VII

All morning I lay down, watching the water and sky and round clouds that had gathered above Maraldina. The sun was bright, air cool, spiders weaving their webs from branch to branch. I fell asleep lying on my stomach so the light wouldn't bother me, the sun beating down on my back. I had perhaps never slept so deeply, so deeply that I was surprised when I awoke. Feeling as if I couldn't sleep, I strolled over to the river and lowered myself into the water, completely, eyes and hair, then I got out. When I reached the center of the seedlings, I noticed the odor of manure and the scent of wisteria blossoms, the two mixed together. I didn't know where the smell came from, everything was so far away, and the river separated us. After the sun and water, it seemed like night beneath the trees. Countless butterflies were fluttering about, many of them resting, wings up, forming white leaves. The axe and pitchfork stood in their usual place; on the ground near the tree trunks lay some nails used to fasten the bark when extracting the seedcase from the tree. I made my way slowly beneath the trees and butterflies, the axe on my back, the awl and pitchfork in my hands. I marked the cross with my fingernail. My nails had grown hard, like my father's. I marked the cross. I wanted to walk about because I was trembling all over. From head to toe. But not because I had moved from the sun into the shade. The trembling sprung from my heart; neither my will nor that of the wind was the cause. Some tiny bones still lay on the stone that had served as a pot. I picked up a few, threw them in the air and let them fall. They were the same color as before, made the same sound as before. Senyor's tree had full leaves and a thick truck. I went over and embraced the trunk, my hands barely able to encircle it. The bee-emblazoned ring was fastened to the base. The fence of thorny

148

brambles had been leveled. I glanced up and was enthralled by the butterflies; then I returned to my tree and began to open up the cross. My heart pounded with each blow of the axe, with each blow. Suddenly I was consumed by fear. Behind me stood the shrub where I had hidden the day my father killed himself, the one with the yellow flower and the furious bee. I leaned down and picked up an old leaf that was full of veins, a web of stiff filaments that had once been tender and clothed in green. I crushed it, then opened my hand and let the pieces fall. I remembered being frightened and hiding behind the shrub as I heard footsteps. It all came back to me. The person who was now unsealing the tree was someone else, and I was hiding behind the shrub. The shadow of two butterflies chasing each other distracted me. I shooed them away and returned to my task of striking the tree with the axe. The trunk was hard. A tree is solid the first time it is split open, but if it has already been breached, it is not difficult to open again. My palms began to sting after a while, and I rested the axe on the ground and spit into them, rubbing one palm against the other. Between two fingers, where the palm hollows out a bit, a blister had formed.

When I had the cross open from top to bottom, I opened it from side to side. I paused and shielded my eyes with my arm. The blister popped, and water oozed out of it; skin was pushed to one side and the raw flesh smarted. A smell emerged from the interior of the tree, like nothing I had ever smelled before. It had a faint trace of something fresh, like a wave that delved deep inside me, compelling me to breathe in what seemed to be a scent of life, enveloped by gasps of smoke, that was coming to me from within the tree.

The butterflies were going mad after flying all day. There seemed to be more and more of them, as if the sun and axe blows were encouraging them to be born and grow faster. Fear returned. Fear caused a drop of salt water to trickle down my back. I had the impression that behind me, where the bee had sucked the flower for so long, a hidden child was watching what I was doing, and the child would run away to alert the villagers, starting with the blacksmith. He would tell them that a man was hollowing out a tree with a pitchfork in the forest of the dead.

I strode over to the shrub. When I had taken four steps, I tripped. One of my feet had caught in the handle of a root, and I hurt my knee. Nothing was behind the shrub. A stream of warm blood ran down my leg. As I turned round to finish opening up the tree, I heard a little laugh, like a memory. On my left cheek, above my heart, I felt a caress mixed with wet hair, as if the air that wasn't air were brushing my cheek with green cane leaves. With a sudden movement, I covered my eyes with my arm, burying the raw flesh from the blister in a fold in my scarred forehead, and I did what I could to keep the caress on my cheek from dying. I took hold of my cheek so the caress would not flee. A ray of sun burnt my chest and dried the blood from my knee. The branches moved. Time was fleeing, and I had to bring Time to a close. Branches swayed, leaves swayed, blades of grass swayed, as if everything that lacked a voice wished to speak to me.

The seedcase rolled out of the tree. I picked up the awl and pointed it at my heart. I was giving them only a corpse. Death without the Festa. I walked back and put away the pitchfork and axe, then returned slowly because my knee ached and the blood that had become a scab pulled with the movement. I gave the seedcase a prod, rolled it to another tree, and covered it with leaves. I hope it will be a long time before they realize. If they drag me from the tree, they will drag me out dead. I removed the four nails from the bark, letting them drop one by one. I pierced my heart with the awl and my life closed. I can begin the story of my life wherever I wish; I can tell it differently, I can begin with the death of my child, with the morning the blacksmith's son jumped in front of me in the forest of the dead, with my visit to Senyor. It matters not what I do, my life is closing. Like a soap bubble that has turned to glass, I cannot remove anything or add anything. I can change nothing in my life. Death escaped through my heart, and when I no longer held death within me, I died.

PENGUIN EUROPEAN WRITERS

THE BEAUTIFUL SUMMER
by Cesare Pavese
With an introduction by Elizabeth Strout

'Life was a perpetual holiday in those days...'

It's the height of summer in 1930s Italy, and sixteen-year-old Ginia is desperate for adventure. So begins a fateful friendship with Amelia, a stylish and sophisticated artist's model who envelops her in a dazzling new world of bohemian artists and intoxicating freedom. Under the spell of her new friends, Ginia soon falls in love with Guido, an enigmatic young painter. It's the start of a desperate love affair, charged with false hope and overwhelming passion - destined to last no longer than the course of a summer.

The Beautiful Summer is a heart-wrenching tale of lost innocence and first love, by one of Italy's greatest writers.

'Pavese, to me, is a constant source of inspiration' Jhumpa Lahiri

'One of the few essential novelists of the mid-twentieth century' Susan Sontag

'There is something about [Pavese] that is insinuating, haunting and lyrically pervasive' *New York Times Book Review*

PENGUIN EUROPEAN WRITERS

THE LADY AND THE LITTLE FOX FUR
by Violette Leduc
With an introduction by Deborah Levy

An old woman lives alone in a tiny attic flat in Paris, counting out coffee beans every morning beneath the roar of the overhead metro. Starving, she spends her days walking around the city, each step a bid for recognition of her own existence. She rides crowded metro carriages to feel the warmth of other bodies, and watches the hot batter of pancakes drip from the hands of street-sellers.

One morning she awakes with an urgent need to taste an orange; but when she rummages in the bins she finds instead a discarded fox fur scarf. The little fox fur becomes the key to her salvation, the friend who changes her lonely existence into a playful world of her own invention.

The Lady and the Little Fox Fur is a stunning portrait of Paris, of the invisibility we all feel in a big city, and ultimately of the hope and triumph of a woman who reclaims her place in the world.

'A forceful affirmation of the human spirit' *Guardian*

'[Leduc] can capture the smells of a country childhood, dazzle with the lights of the Place de la Concorde or make you feel the silky slither of her eel-grey suit' *Observer*

'This book is as richly humane as anything else you're likely to read' *Independent*